RAY'S LEGACY

Ray's Legacy

P. R. PAGE

Copyright © 2024 P. R. Page

The moral right of the author has been asserted.

Apart from any fair dealing for the purposes of research or private study, or criticism or review, as permitted under the Copyright, Designs and Patents Act 1988, this publication may only be reproduced, stored or transmitted, in any form or by any means, with the prior permission in writing of the publishers, or in the case of reprographic reproduction in accordance with the terms of licences issued by the Copyright Licensing Agency. Enquiries concerning reproduction outside those terms should be sent to the publishers.

This is a work of fiction. Names, characters, businesses, places, events and incidents are either the products of the author's imagination or used in a fictitious manner. Any resemblance to actual persons, living or dead, or actual events is purely coincidental.

Matador
Unit E2 Airfield Business Park,
Harrison Road, Market Harborough,
Leicestershire. LE16 7UL
Tel: 0116 2792299
Email: books@troubador.co.uk
Web: www.troubador.co.uk/matador
Twitter: @matadorbooks

ISBN 978 1805141 846

British Library Cataloguing in Publication Data.
A catalogue record for this book is available from the British Library.

Printed and bound in Great Britain by 4edge Limited
Typeset in 10.5pt Palatino by Troubador Publishing Ltd, Leicester, UK

Matador is an imprint of Troubador Publishing Ltd

For Rob Berry
With love

Acknowledgements

My eternal thanks to Lorraine Dilks, who very kindly typed and edited this book for me and guided me through the legal procedures. Thanks also to Eddie, her husband who kept my computer functioning.

I would not have achieved it without their invaluable help.

To Kari McGowan, I am thrilled with the cover you have so expertly designed for my book. I am completely in awe at the lovely picture you have created.

Thank so you so much.

Chapter One

James opened the door to the summer house and swore loudly as he tripped on the threshold, sending his pencils and sketch book flying across the floor. He quickly picked himself up and looked out of the window at his two young sisters playing in the garden. It appeared they hadn't heard what he'd said, thank God. His parents would be less than pleased if the girls repeated his words!

He retrieved his sketch pad and pencils, sat down, and glanced out of the window again; his mother was in the garden, laughing at the antics of Cassie and Katie as she stroked her stomach slowly and tenderly. Startled, James sat upright, thinking, she's pregnant! Mum is pregnant! He remembered her doing that when she was expecting the twins. She looked happy and quite lovely. He was surprised at his own thoughts and quickly sketched the scene he witnessed through the window. Felicity caught hold of the twins and went into the cottage while James drew frantically before he lost the image from his mind.

Half an hour later he surveyed his work, pleased and astounded at the result. It was the best drawing he had ever done. He'd captured the air of happiness and joy surrounding his mother perfectly, the sparkle in her eyes and the look of pure enchantment on her face. The twins were playing in the background, and the whole scene emanated serenity and joyfulness.

James shook himself, almost embarrassed by his own perceptions. He gathered his things together and rushed from the summer house, having remembered he was supposed to be helping to dig the kitchen garden. He rushed into the house and through the kitchen, went into his room and hid the sketch book carefully in his laptop case. Quite why, he wasn't sure; he just wanted to keep it private. He locked the door after he left the room and pocketed the key; it was the first time he'd ever locked it since he'd moved in there.

He was two weeks from his fourteenth birthday when Felicity had given birth to the twins. He'd been three years old when she'd had her first miscarriage; her second followed when he was ten. Two more followed in the next two years, and then the twins arrived six weeks early. The cottage had three bedrooms: one was Felicity's own sitting room, dominated by her painting of Simon; another was his parents' room; and the third was his own. When the twins were six months old, they held a family conference and offered James one of the two rooms opposite the kitchen. He was delighted; it had doors to the garden and was big enough for him to have a proper computer desk plus his bedroom furniture.

He'd helped to plan the layout and decorate it, making it into his own small domain.

As he walked out to the garden, he wondered if he would have to share it if Mum had a baby boy; he was so used to his own space that he didn't relish the thought of perhaps having to share it.

He decided he would ask Dad.

Chapter Two

Felicity heard the key turn in the lock of James's room as he went to join his father in the garden and raised her eyebrows in surprise. He'd never done that before, but she wouldn't pry; after all, he was a young man now, being nearly sixteen. She smiled and turned back to the twins, who were settled at the table with their biscuits and drinks.

She sat down opposite them and smiled, her eyes glowing with love and sheer delight because she was ecstatic at being pregnant again. She felt so well, and it was past the danger period when she'd previously miscarried. She knew exactly when this baby had been conceived. It was when she'd decided to clear out her kitchen cupboards on the morning the twins were at playschool and James was at school. Just as she was backing out from the cupboard under the sink, she banged her head. While sitting on the floor, rubbing her head, she raised her eyes to see a pair of boots in her eyeline; a memory had stirred, and she let out a peal of laughter. Simon held out his hand to her, as he'd done so many years ago, but this time, he held on to her, not letting her go. He gathered her to him, and she melted into his arms. He scooped her up, carried her upstairs into her sitting room and laid her on the carpet.

Gently, lovingly and tenderly, he made love to her, undressing her slowly and caressing her with his hands and mouth. She reciprocated his desire and love in every touch and move. Their world was their own; it was just the two of them, enfolded, entwined and entrenched in each other, culminating in a passionate explosion of love.

They lay quietly together for a while, until she sat up suddenly, exclaiming "Simon, I must collect the twins from playschool, otherwise Jeannie will be knocking at the door with them, wondering where I am". She started to gather her clothes, Simon touched her arm quietly, saying, "Wait, Felicity; wait a moment."

She stopped and looked questioningly at him.

He was searching in the pocket of his jeans and then he held out his hand; a small rectangular box was lying in the palm of his hand. "I was going to save this to give to you at a special moment, I think that moment is now."

She dropped her clothes and took the box from him. When she opened it, her eyes widened in surprise and wonder. She withdrew a pendant suspended on a beautiful gold chain. The oval pendant had two miniature pictures enclosed in a delicate gold mount that matched the chain. One side had a picture of the cottage, Simon's Fel in its derelict state; the other was of Simon's Fel when it had been restored. With her eyes glistening, she looked at Simon questioningly.

"I wanted to give you something really special, so I had this made especially. It comes with all my love," he said, and then he went across to her, took it from her hands and fastened it around her neck. It was beautiful.

He drew in his breath sharply as she still had the power to make his heart pound and his desire and love for her grow more each day each year. He groaned and gathered her in his arms again. Playschool forgotten, she fell into his arms, her whole body tingling and trembling. He kissed her, his eyes glinting with those incredible silver specks.

The doorbell rang. Simon cursed loudly and dashed from the room, leaving Felicity swaying and trembling, her legs unable to support her. Simon grabbed his dressing gown from their room, ran downstairs and opened the door to Jeannie, who'd brought the twins home.

She opened her mouth to ask if Felicity was OK, but then realised in a split second, from seeing Simon's attire and the look in his incredible eyes as to why she hadn't collected the twins. However, she quickly ushered them in through the door, saying, "Would you please tell Felicity I'll call her later this afternoon". She smiled, but as she turned to go Simon stopped her.

"Jeannie, I want to thank you. I gave Felicity the pendant; it's so lovely, and I couldn't have got it made forty your help. She looks beautiful; it's perfect for her.

Thank you so much". He crushed her in a bear hug, then abruptly turned around and closed the door.

The twins had disappeared upstairs and were surprised to find Mummy sitting on the floor in her room, not quite fully dressed, smiling and crying at the same time, her fingers stroking the pendant nestling against her chest.

"Mummy, Mummy!" the twins exclaimed together, bringing Felicity out of her reverie and back to the present. "We've finished; look it's all gone".

"OK, you guys, off to your room and play quietly, Mummy has to get dinner ready".

The girls scampered out, and Felicity sat still for a few moments, her mind on their baby. *Tonight,* she decided, *tonight, I will tell Simon.*

*

Returning her thoughts to the present day, she shook her head, drew her attention back to the twins, and moved towards the sink and the pile of vegetables to prepare for dinner.

Tonight, she decided, I will tell Simon.

Chapter Three

Simon, meanwhile, was happily digging the kitchen garden, grudgingly helped by James. Although James wasn't too enamoured with having to do this job, he was doing all right and keeping pace with his father. Simon was proud of James; he was a good boy – well, young man now. He rebelled occasionally, but he mostly did as he was asked and was above average at school. He'd inherited his mother's love of art and was exceptionally good at it. He always had a sketch pad with him and had produced some excellent work.

One thing that concerned Simon was James's interest in law – he'd expressed a desire to follow this profession. That had sparked a frown of disapproval from Simon, fuelled by his own disastrous upbringing and unhappy childhood. His father and late half-brother had been lawyers, so he hated the profession with a passion and didn't want his son going down that road. He begrudgingly realised he was being totally unreasonable and selfish, but he couldn't separate the two.

He leant on his spade and watched James. His son really was a mixture of the two of them; perhaps he should take notice of that and trust that the boy would remain the product of his and Felicity's genes and not those of his grandfather and late uncle. Sighing, his brow furrowed with thinking about the problem, he attacked the garden with increased fervour, taking his frustration out on the ground.

James watched his father, not sure what was bothering him, but he knew there was conflict in his father's attitude. He too sighed and continued digging, his mind also wrestling with a problem. Abruptly, he stopped, leant on his spade, took a deep breath and began to speak. "Dad," he said, breaking into Simon's thoughts, "Dad, when's Mum's baby due?"

Chapter Four

Simon's foot slipped off the spade at James's words. He was astounded at the question. Baby? What baby? Felicity hasn't mentioned anything; she's not even given a sign nor shown any symptoms. What on earth is James talking about?

All these thoughts flashed across his mind in a few seconds before he realised James had stopped digging and was looking at him quizzically.Gathering his scattered thoughts, Simon smiled shakily and said, "We should have realised you might have guessed; after all, you're approaching sixteen". He stopped to take a breath. "We were waiting to be sure everything was OK before we told you". *But now you appear to know more than I do,* he thought bitterly. *Why hasn't she told me?* He was getting angry, surprised at how hurt he felt that his son knew before he did. He shook himself and then realised that James hadn't been told by Felicity – he'd just worked it out. *Why hadn't I noticed?* he asked himself, experience should surely have made him more perceptive.

He looked over at James, who was continuing to dig, seemingly happy with his Dad's answer. The boy was growing up fast; he was in his last year at school and soon to start college. A young man, very much with the same temperament as his father, but with Felicity's sensitivity.

"Come on, James; I think we'll stop for today.Let's finish this tomorrow". suggested Simon.

He walked away to the tool shed, shaking, still angry at both himself and Felicity, and trying not to convey this feeling to James.They cleared away their tools and went inside.

Felicity was humming while she tidied the kitchen as they entered. James went to his room, and Simon stood watching Felicity as she bustled about; the twins were nowhere to be seen. Simon assumed they were having their daytime nap. Taking a deep breath and holding down his feeling of anger, he went across to Felicity and gently turned her around to face him.

"Why haven't you told me?" he asked. "Why didn't you share this with me? Why keep it from me?"

His grip had tightened on her arms and his eyes had darkened, but then, as she reached up to caress his cheek, her smile lit up her whole face, silver glints appeared in his eyes, and they softened into desire for her. He enfolded her into his body, then picked her up and carried her to their room. He laid her on the bed and restrained himself from making love to her; he had to know about the baby."Tell me, Felicity, tell me about the baby".

"I wanted to be sure Simon; I didn't want to tell you until I was sure. I had a scan yesterday, and everything is fine. It was the second scan and our baby is due around mid-November. There's no problem; everything is as it should be. I'm fine, and the baby is developing properly, so we should have no worries at all. Oh, and there's only one this time!"

"Are you sure, darling? Are you really sure?" He hugged her to him again and then said, "James asked me in the garden when the baby was due. I nearly fell over. He's guessed you were pregnant. He's very observant."

Felicity pulled away from him, surprised by Simon's words. "How did he know? What made him think that?"

"I don't know; I haven't asked him, but I will. Our son is growing up, much more than I realised. I should be more reasonable and let him make his own decision about his future." Simon got up from the bed, smiled at Felicity and went to find James.

Felicity continued to sit on the bed and thought about Simon's words. She was genuinely surprised that James had guessed she was pregnant. She too would ask their son just how he'd found out. He was indeed growing up, but why had Simon suddenly been serious about James's future? Her sensitivity to Simon's moods had alerted her to something deeper that he hadn't mentioned.

Chapter Five

Felicity slowly got up from the bed and went to the window; she stood there for a while, then sighed heavily and turned to go downstairs. For the first time in years, she felt vulnerable and somewhat lonely. She shook herself, what was the matter with her, why these feelings now? She'd no need to feel this way: life was good, she loved her husband, and they had three beautiful children and another on the way. Why the disquiet in her mind and soul? Once more, she shook her head to clear it of these unwelcome thoughts. Taking a deep breath, she put a smile on her face as she walked downstairs.

Just as she reached the bottom step, James's door opened, and Simon came out of the room, followed closely by James, who had a big smile on his face. He walked towards his mother as she stood on the staircase. "Mum, Dad has agreed I can study law, so I'm going to take the options at Sixth Form College to start preparing for university; hopefully, to get into the best one for a career in law!" He gave her a huge hug and dashed off to who knows where. He was literally bouncing as he went out the front door.

Simon hadn't moved from the door to James's room; he looked drained and almost as though he could cry.

Felicity quickly went to him and put her arms around him, burying her head in his chest. "Thank you, Simon; thank you so much, darling. You've made James so happy." She looked up at Simon, her eyes shining with love and happiness. Her breath caught in her throat; she was taken back almost to the day they'd met, when he'd looked at her in the same way, his beautiful, dark eyes with the silver specks. It was as if he could look deep into her soul.

She reached up and stroked his cheek with her hand: "It's OK, Simon; it will be OK. Nothing can happen now, you've made sure nothing could ever happen to our cottage."

Surprised at her own words, she realised instinctively it was the cottage Simon was worried about. His half-brother had been about to become a barrister when he'd died in a road accident. A cruel and violent man, Simon had vowed he would never let his half-brother's family get the cottage that he and Felicity had fought over. He had given it to her for their son, trusting their good friend Ray to make sure it was watertight legally and could never be revoked. Although, at the back of his mind, he'd always felt that some clever lawyer could wheedle their way round it and take it from them. And now his son wanted to be a lawyer! Simon hated lawyers and their profession with an intense passion. His father and grandfather had been lawyers, and he'd broken that mould, but now he'd agreed to let his son follow that path. He had a deeply entrenched feeling that disaster loomed ahead.

Felicity watched as the expression on Simon's face changed: his eyes turned a darker, stormy grey, with the silver glint almost luminescent. Once more, Felicity froze, not breathing. Time had stopped; it seemed as though they were caught in a void and nothing would ever penetrate it. The moment was lost as one of the twins cried out. Both Simon and Felicity jumped at the sound, trembling from the intensity of the last few minutes.

"Come on, Felicity, my love," Simon said, "Let's go and get the twins." He grabbed her hand and moved to go upstairs. Swiftly, he pulled her into his arms, kissed her deeply, then smiled and whispered, "I love you and our new little one."

Happily, they went to retrieve the twins, who were both now shouting for Mummy and Daddy. An unspoken agreement had been reached between them; words had not been necessary. They both knew they would fight as one to keep their home and family together and safe from any harm – no matter what threatened them.

Sometime later, Felicity asked James how he'd known she was pregnant. He explained about watching her with the twins and how he'd guessed by the smile on her face and the way she was happily stroking her stomach. They were sitting together in the garden, talking quietly about his move to Sixth Form College to prepare for a university degree followed by a career in law. She was amazed at his confidence that he would achieve his goal. He really had grown up so much in a short space of time and was adamant he could be successful.

"Wait there, Mum, I have something I want to show you." James jumped up from his chair, ran indoors and, a few moments later, came back with the picture he'd sketched. He shyly handed it to her and waited for her comments.

"James, it's beautiful!", she exclaimed. "May I keep it?", as she looked at James, tears were springing to her eyes.

"I drew it for you and Dad. I was just waiting for the right moment to give it to you." He gave her a quick hug, muttered, "I have some studying to do," then went off towards the summer house, pleased that the right moment had come to give it to her at last. Things were working out so well at the moment: his plans for college were settled, Dad had given consent for his chosen career, Mum was really well, and life was good!

*

Simon had resigned himself to James wanting to study law, although he kept his reservations to himself. He couldn't shake off his deep distrust of lawyers, but he tried hard to hide it from Felicity and James. His main concern though, was for Felicity and their baby. He prayed that all would go well, but he worried constantly. He saw James go into the summer house, and then Simon wandered round the garden to where Felicity had been sitting with James while he'd been weeding.

Felicity was looking at a picture; she looked up at Simon as he approached. "Look at this. James just gave it to me. He drew it! Isn't it lovely? We must frame it."

Simon took the picture from her and was astounded that James had drawn such a lovely picture. He'd captured the expression on Felicity's face perfectly: the serenity, joy and happiness shining from her. The joyfulness of the twins as they played beside her added to the sketch to make it the perfect family picture.

Simon knelt down beside her, gathered her into his arms and kissed her lovingly. "This picture will have pride of place in the sitting room. It's excellent, and you look even more beautiful than ever."

He called to the twins to come over so he could show them the picture. They did so and were amazed to see themselves; they jumped up and down with excitement.

Laughing at their antics, Simon and Felicity took them both indoors, and they all went into the sitting room to decide on the best place to hang it.

Life for them all was quietly moving along, but Simon was still worrying and fretting about the baby and his son's choice of career.

Chapter Six

Jeannie rushed over as soon as Felicity had called her. She went straight round to the kitchen door, opened it and called out, "Where are you, Felicity?"

"In the living room Jeannie; please come quickly!" There was panic in Felicity's voice, and the twins were crying.

Not knowing what was wrong, Jeannie took charge as soon as she went in because she realised immediately that Felicity was in labour. She was on the floor, her back against the sofa, breathing evenly and deeply, holding her sides as the contractions took hold.

"Come on, Katie and Cassie, I've got chocolate biscuits and lemonade," said Jeannie, and then she grabbed them, ushered them into the kitchen and quickly sat them at the table with biscuits and drinks. "Stay there, girls, and don't move until I come back. I won't be long."

The twins nodded, smiling happily at the unexpected treat of lemonade.

Once back in the living room, Jeannie raised her eyes questioningly at Felicity and, having received a quick nod in reply, phoned Ray Luxton, who was now in his mid-seventies and retired.

"Ray, can you come to Felicity's, collect the twins, take them back to my house and help Abe with them all? Felicity's in labour." Jeannie then rang off without waiting for an answer, then immediately dialled 999 for an ambulance.

Quickly, she turned to Felicity, who was now groaning and trying hard not to push as the contractions got stronger. "How far apart are they?"

Felicity put up three fingers as she was unable to talk.

Damn, thought Jeannie, *I hope the ambulance arrives soon.* She knelt down at Felicity's side and asked where Simon was.

"Mobile," Felicity gasped, "Phone his mobile."

Once more, Jeannie grabbed the phone and called Simon's number. There was no answer; it went to voicemail. Jeannie just stated, "Baby's coming," and broke off the contact.

"Quick, Jeannie, quick; I'm sure the baby is coming." Felicity managed to say.

She was now lying on the floor, and Jeannie grabbed some cushions, put them under Felicity's head, mouthed at her that she would be back in a moment and dashed into the kitchen just as Ray arrived.

"Thank God. Ray, please just take the twins away and give them anything they want." She was gathering some towels as she spoke to Ray." I've called an ambulance. It may not arrive in time, but between the two of us we will manage – after all, we do have six children between us. Off you go with, Pops, girls; Bella and the others are waiting for you." She smiled at Ray, leaving him to sort the girls out and went back to Felicity.

She was only just in time. As she got to Felicity's side, the baby was half born, and with another push, he slid out into the world. Jeannie caught him deftly, wrapped him in a towel, gave him to Felicity and went to sterilise some scissors to cut the cord.

She'd just grabbed the scissors from the drawer when she saw the paramedics hurrying down the path. Abandoning her task, she opened the door and said, "The baby came a couple of minutes ago, the cord needs to be cut and the rest, I think, you'll know. Felicity is on the floor in there with a new son."

The paramedics nodded and went to Felicity's aid. Jeannie sat down quickly on the nearest chair, aware she'd become a bit giddy; however, she looked up as she heard Simon calling as he rushed down the garden path. The door crashed open, and Jeannie just pointed to the living room.

Tears sprang to her eyes, happy tears; happy for Felicity and Simon – for the whole family. The phone rang, startling her, and she jumped up to answer it. It was Abe calling to be sure everything was OK.

"Yes, we are, my love; we are. Felicity and Simon have another son, isn't that wonderful?" She laughed at the raucous sounds in the background. "What on earth is going on?"

"Pops is pretending to be a big horse, and they're taking turns to have a ride; they're currently trying to find out how many of them can sit on him at once."

Jeannie laughed again and told Abe she would be home very soon. How she loved him; she always had. She still smiled at the memory of how he'd literally knocked her off her feet, and she'd loved him from that moment.

She got up from the chair, and as she did so, the door opened again.

James rushed in asking, "Who's hurt, AJ? Why's there an ambulance out there? Is it Mum or one of the twins?"

"Your Mum's had the baby; you have a brother."

"But it wasn't due yet; is she OK? A brother, you said – are you sure?"

"Yes, James, I'm sure." She smiled at the expression on his face. He really was growing up – a real young adult now.

"May I see him and Mum, please?" he asked.

He made to go into the living room, and Jeannie was about to stop him when the door opened and Simon came out, carrying his baby son.

"This is your new baby brother; would you like to hold him?" Simon asked.

James dropped his school bags and gently took his baby brother from his dad. He'd held his sisters when they'd been babies and had no hesitation in holding him.

Simon was smiling hugely. His eyes glinted with the silver flecks that were so unique to him, but so expressive and enlightening.He grabbed Jeannie in a bear hug and muttered, "Thank you, thank you so much."

"I must go and rescue Abe and Pops from the children; I just abandoned them." She extricated herself from his embrace and turned to go. "Congratulations to you all; he is lovely, and I'm proud to have been able to help.

"Dad, take my brother, please. I'll go with AJ and bring the twins back." James then handed the baby to his father and happily went off with Jeannie.

They'd always got on well, and from quite a young age, he had got into the habit of calling her "AJ".He hadn't quite got his tongue around Auntie Jeannie, so he'd come up with "AJ"– though how or why they didn't really know. But it had stuck and Jeannie enjoyed it. After all, her husband was known by his initials, so why shouldn't she be?

James stayed at Jeannie's for a couple of hours. She'd phoned Simon and said she would feed them all to save him the trouble as he'd have enough to do sorting out everything for Felicity and the little one. They explained to Cassie and Katie that they had a new baby brother, and James added that they would see him when they got home.

*

That evening, by 9pm saw the twins in bed, having been shown their little brother; Felicity was asleep, with the baby in the crib beside her; and James and Simon were sitting in the now tidy living room, relaxing after clearing up and putting the excited twins to bed.

Simon stood up suddenly, went into the kitchen and returned with two small glasses of whisky. "I think we should toast the baby and your mother. I'm proud of you, James; you've been a tremendous help today. Thank you." He gave James one of the glasses and took a sip from his.

James followed suit, coughed on the whisky and, still spluttering, said, "Thanks, Dad; I'm honoured to share this with you, but you can finish it!" He smiled at his Dad, handed him the glass, then turned and went to go to bed.

At the door, he turned back. "I won't ever let you down, Dad."

Chapter Seven

Ray had continued to live above the Estate Agency after his wife had died. The couple who had bought the business from him five years ago had their own house in Middle Trenchard and didn't need the flat Ray occupied. The new owners were happy for Ray to remain there, legal papers were drawn up to ensure he had the right to reside above the Agency for the rest of his life.

Life was good for him, although he missed his wife still, but he was settled in the flat as it held many memories for him – treasured memories. He still occasionally looked after the Estate Agency for the current owners when they took a break for a few days, which he enjoyed enormously, but he was happy in his retirement, loved his adopted family and was content with his way of life.

He knew with certainty that he had a home for his remaining years, good friends and a peaceful existence, which was made even more enjoyable by the children to whom he was an adopted "Granddad".

After being with Abe, Jeannie and the children for dinner and James had t taken the twins home, he had gone home too. He settled back in his chair, feeling very tired, probably as a result from acting as a horse for the twins!

The children had all adopted him as their Grandfather (none of them had a grandfather on either side of the family) and all called him "Pops". This had come about when young Bella copied his habit of saying, "I'll pop over." She'd said to her mother one day, as she saw Ray walking down their path, "Here comes Pops, Mummy," and it had stuck.

He loved his nickname and adored all the children; he and his wife had sadly never had any of their own. How they had all grown! Bella was training to be a nurse and Sebastian, who was hoping to become an accountant, was soon to start university.

James wanted to be a lawyer. Ray had seen the tension between him and his father and he'd tried to get Simon to see that his objections were bordering on the obsessive and selfish to boot. His relationship with Simon had grown and deepened since the marriage of Felicity and Simon. They were very close, and Ray had become Felicity's adopted father. James was sensitive and artistic, both traits he had inherited from his mother. He could be stubborn, though, and had great depths, both traits of his father. Ray sighed. He did hope Simon would mellow in his attitude to James's career choice. He worried, though, as he knew why Simon was so against it, which wasn't an easy thing to explain to

James. Did he need to know? Not really. Ray thought best to let sleeping dogs lie.

Ray sighed again as he got up to replenish his glass. He was getting old, he decided: his joints ached and he was a bit breathless. He would be glad to get to get to bed. It had been too much exertion playing with the children; after all, he wasn't getting any younger! He shook off his depressing thoughts and returned his mind to more pleasant subjects.

Now settled back in his chair with his glass of whisky and a smile on his face at the thought of his new adopted grandchild, he had no idea about the trauma and tragedy that would arise from James's career choice.

Chapter Eight

Abe sat watching Jeannie; she looked exhausted, but was smiling happily, her eyes closed as she relaxed. His heart lurched; she was a lovely looking woman and had given him such happiness. He reached out and touched her hand.

She immediately enfolded her hand in his, her smile widening. "I'm not asleep; just thinking of Simon and Felicity's baby. He's beautiful and was born so quickly. He's just lovely, just as though he was a few weeks old."

She opened her eyes, and Abe read the question in them.

His fingers tightened on hers, and he said gently, "I'm nearly sixty-seven; isn't that really too old to be having another baby? We have three wonderful children; isn't that enough?"

Jeannie looked down for a few moments, knowing in her heart that he was right but not wanting to acknowledge it. She sighed, extricated her hand from his and went to sit on his lap. She snuggled into him and whispered that she agreed with him; she could always babysit for Felicity and Simon.

They sat there for a while until Bella came in from her late duty at the hospital in Plymouth. Oblivious to her parents sitting engrossed in each other, she suddenly said, "Anything to eat, Mum?"

Jeannie started to get up, but Abe stopped her, held her tight to him, and said to his eldest: "Your mother acted as midwife to Felicity today, so you'll have to get yourself something. I'm taking her to bed."

Bella looked up astonished as her father scooped her mother up in his arms from his lap and carried her upstairs.

Good Lord! thought Bella, *They're far too old to be acting like that.* She dismissed the thought and went to raid the fridge. Bella suddenly realised what her father had said as she'd got home. Midwife to Felicity?! She must have had the baby! But it was too early! She dashed out of the kitchen and was halfway to her parent's room when she stopped, realisation dawning on her that now was probably not an appropriate moment to disturb them.

She returned to the kitchen to collect her thoughts. She would wait a while and then phone Simon and Felicity, Pops too; they would all be so pleased. Bella, happy for them all, decided she would tell Seb about the baby when he got home. She had lots to talk to him about – ideas were forming in her mind that needed clarification and some of them required his agreement.

While she was eating the omelette she'd made

herself, she decided that she must have a serious discussion with her brother immediately. When Janine was six years old and Bella had just turned sixteen, their parents decided to extend the house. Abe had demolished the double garage at the side of the house and built a two-storey extension along the whole side. Half the ground floor had been made back into a double garage, and the other half was turned into a small sitting room and kitchenette with its own access door. The whole top storey, which was accessed by stairs from the living room, had been turned into two very large bedrooms, both en suite. The staircase was in the centre and it had a door at the top that gave access to the main house.

This change was made as Bella had needed to share a room with Janine; Sebastian, as the only boy, had the third bedroom. Abe had built it himself with the aid of Stan and Dave, who'd worked for him since they started in the construction business.

When it had been completed, Bella and Seb moved in; firstly, just into the top floor, using the access from the main house. After Bella had turned eighteen and Seb was nearly sixteen, Abe and Jeannie decided they were ready for some responsibility and could use the other access. The sitting room and kitchenette were fitted out, and they became self-sufficient. Well, almost – they still ate with the family and their Mum still did all their washing.

Now, though, Bella decided she and Seb should fend for themselves, more or less completely as, after all, they had everything they needed.

As if on cue, Seb walked in, and Bella immediately told him about the baby and then her ideas.

"Great," Seb replied, thinking he could then have friends round, parties and girlfriends, of course, all went through his mind!

I'll ask Dad tomorrow, Bella decided, *and get Stan to do the work.* She knew he was seventeen years older than her, but she also knew he was the man for her. They'd always been friends, and she'd fallen in love with him when he'd come to her eighteenth birthday party. She was sure he was attracted to her. She smiled, unaware it was exactly the same smile her mother had when she thought of Bella's father.

Seb went off, whistling happily at Bella's idea, his sights going no further than games nights and sports evenings, watching the TV with his mates and –of course – girls! He reached for his mobile to ring James about his new brother and to let him know of their plans.

Bella took her tea into their sitting room, closed her eyes and let her thoughts drift to Stan. How she loved him! She would make sure he was aware of her; she was a grown adult now, confident of her feelings, and she wanted to be with him always. She sat up abruptly *.What will Mum and Dad say? Nothing! What reasons can they have to object? After all, Mum's twenty years younger than Dad!* She smiled widely – life was good!

Chapter Nine

It had been a difficult few weeks since the baby had arrived. Many visits had been made to the hospital and many tests had to be arranged. Their son had developed breathing problems, but fortunately, it was all due to his premature birth. However, he was declared fit and well after a few weeks, with no permanent damage.

Jeannie had invited the whole family to visit her for the day so Felicity could have the day to herself, with only herself and the baby to worry about.

It was a blessed relief for Felicity, as she was exhausted and hadn't realised how tired she was until the hospital had discharged their baby son. She smiled happily at him as he lay in his pram, peaceful and fast asleep. She sat down and took the opportunity to catch up on her sleep, knowing that Jeannie was entertaining the whole family meant she had a completely free day to herself.

When the family came home later that day, Simon could immediately see that Felicity was looking better. The worry had gone from her face, she was settled and back to her serene self. It was so good to see. Even the twins were happier, as they could sense the relief in her manner.

Having got the twins to bed, the baby settled in his cot and James ensconced in his room, Simon and Felicity went to bed, knowing the past few weeks were behind them and they could settle happily into the future.

*

The following morning, when the family had all left for work or school, Felicity knew they must decide on a name for the baby. Simon, Ray, James, Jeannie, Abe, and even Lucy and Michael (still the landlords of The Tavern in Little Trenchard) had made several suggestions. It was a chance meeting with Mrs Carlyon (who had bought the Estate Agency from Ray) that gave Felicity the idea for a name. After admiring the baby, Mrs Carlyon went on her way after telling Felicity that, every time she went to value a property, she had to drive miles to get there as she hadn't realised at first how many miles of roads there were in Devon.

Myles, thought Felicity as she pushed the pram along the road on her way to collect the twins from playschool. *Myles Grantley. Yes, I like it. I'll call Simon when we're back home.* She must also discuss with him where the baby would go when he was old enough to move from their room. She'd been thinking about it for a while and was sure her plan could work; she would talk about it to Simon later.

However, she didn't get time to ring Simon after collecting the twins as they were tetchy and naughty all afternoon; they just wouldn't rest up. The baby sensed the tension in the air and grizzled alongside the twins. When James got home from college, he banged his door shut and yelled that he couldn't study with all the noise going on.

That's it, thought Felicity, *I must persuade Simon that we have to carry out my idea.* It had now turned into a definite plan in her mind.

---
*

She was exhausted by the time he came home. When dinner was over, the twins were now quiet and asleep in their beds, and James was watching sport in his room, Felicity broached the subject. Simon was looking through some paperwork in readiness for his next job.

"Simon, please stop. I need to talk to you; it's important." She'd fed the baby, who was almost asleep, so now was the opportunity.

"What is it, darling? Are you OK? You look really tired." He sat down beside her and gathered her into his arms; she felt so good as he rested his chin on her hair.

"How about the name Myles for the baby? Myles Grantley sounds good."

Simon sat up straight, his head to one side as he considered it. "Yes," he said, "I like it; it's a great name,

Myles it is." He smiled, pleased Felicity had thought of it.

"Oh good; that's great. I have something else I need to discuss with you too."

Simon listened as Felicity outlined her plans. The girls would move into James's room. It was bigger than their current one, so they could have single beds not bunk beds, each would have their own wardrobe and chest for their clothes, plus there would be space for their toys too. Myles would eventually move into the twins' room, and James could move into the new room they would build. As Simon opened his mouth to speak, Felicity put her fingers on his lips to stop him speaking and asked him to wait until she'd finished.

She continued, "We could replace the summer house with a proper cabin, all insulated, with a small en suite shower room and toilet. He could have a sort of bedsit with space for his computer desk, TV and bed, plus a small settee. We could fit wardrobe space over and around his bed, and he could come over to the cottage for meals. As it is, we rarely see him now; he seems to only join us for meals as he spends the rest of the time in his room. What do you think?"

Simon leant back on the sofa, his mind whirling with questions and thoughts. It was basically a good idea, but could they afford it? Was he too young to be away from the house? *Stop that,* he told himself. *Remember where you were at that age!* It would give all the children their own space and would make studying for James easier. "Couldn't we turn your sitting room …." Felicity interrupted him. "No, we couldn't; that room is sacrosanct, and it is *not* available for change." She was adamant about that. It was far too significant in her life to be altered – too much had happened there.

Simon smiled, understanding her outburst fully. Gathering her to him again, he said, "OK, my love; we'll plan it properly and cost it out. We could certainly use the foundations under the summerhouse and maybe some of the wood as well. We'll make plans and then talk to James. It will be a big step for him, so he must be involved. And tomorrow morning, we'll introduce the three of them formally to Myles."

Chapter Ten

It took a few weeks to get their plans for James's cabin ready. Simon went to see Abe for advice as well as asking if he was available to help build it; they'd become firm friends since James was born and built up a great deal of trust between them.

Delighted to be involved, Abe did most of the research into which cabin would be the most suitable. They had information on three different styles and decided to let James pick the one he wanted.

Ray was a huge help, steering them through any planning difficulties that arose. Felicity worried about him, though. He didn't seem to have as much energy lately and was often tired. However, he'd insisted he was OK, just passing it off as being only due to old age. Felicity resolved to keep an eye on him.

Abe contacted Stan and Dave (who had completed their apprenticeships with him) to see if they could assist with the building of the new cabin. They were thrilled to be involved; they often did work locally and were well-known and trusted workmen. He knew too that his daughter Bella would be very pleased to know Stan was involved; she was, and had been for a long time, very fond of him. Stan and Dave would both be an important part of the planning and building; they'd both been a big part in all their lives.

Felicity and Simon decided that, when they had all the information, they'd throw a small party and present the plan to James. Felicity asked Jeannie, Bella, Seb, Janine, Stan and Dave to come with Abe. Ray had also been invited; he was so much a part of their families.

Six weeks after Felicity had first announced her idea to Simon, they were all gathered in the living room at Simon's Fel; apart from Simon, Felicity, Abe and Jeannie, no one knew why there was this impromptu party. James had rebelled over being there, but Simon had insisted, telling him how he would upset his mother if he didn't join in. Rather reluctantly, he gave in and was astonished when Simon quietened everyone and addressed him directly.

"James, this party is for you. Your mother had the excellent idea of building you your own cabin in the garden. It will be almost completely self-sufficient. All you need to do is decide which one you would like; the rest is in place for us to begin building next week." He stopped speaking and handed James a large folder plus three brochures.

Somewhat embarrassed at being the centre of attention, James took the bundle of papers, turned to his Mother and declared, "Thanks, Mum." He smiled at Felicity and then turning to his Dad he said: "You too, Dad. Will you come with me to help me decide?"

Simon nodded and followed James as he went to his own room.

"Why are they going, Mummy? What are they doing?" Cassie asked.

Felicity smiled at her and explained they were looking at plans for James's new cabin in the garden.

Questions flowed from the children, all of them wanting to know why, when, what for and whether they would have one too. Laughter filled the rooms as the endless questions went on, with Ray, Jeannie and Abe joining in with the banter. Stan and Dave soon realised what a happy family they were and joined in too!

Jeannie went to help Felicity with the buffet supper they'd prepared and she offered her help if needed. Myles woke up crying to be fed, so Jeannie was left to help everyone to food while Felicity fed him.

It wasn't long before James and Simon reappeared, the choice having been made with some minor changes to the layout suggested by James. He was stunned but thrilled to be getting his own almost fully independent space. He'd asked his Dad to incorporate a large window at the far end of the cabin and to fit a desk there for him to indulge his love of sketching. Simon was happy to agree, feeling pleased and proud that James was involving himself to such an extent. He would obviously be content there; he already seemed to have matured since being told of their idea.

---
*

Simon and Abe started work two days later, dismantling the summer house and checking the foundations were sufficient to support the new building. The cabin was due to arrive in two weeks' time, so they worked hard to ensure all the groundwork was completed prior to the delivery.

Abe arranged for Stan and Dave to assist them with the building and fitting out when the cabin arrived. They rearranged their current jobs so that at least one of them could be available to assist Simon and Abe most of the time.

The work was progressing steadily; Abe mostly project managed the work, with Simon and Stan working under his direction and Dave helping when he was able to. Abe was quietly watching the growing attachment between Bella and Stan; she came round most days when she was off duty, always with a smile for Stan and offers of drinks and cake if they were ready for a break. Abe made a mental note to mention the growing attachment to Jeannie when he got home!

James assisted them on most days when he returned from school; he was eager to do so as part of his way of saying thank you to his parents for their gift. He decided he would have a moving-in party, with help from his Mum, of course!

Chapter Eleven

A few days later, work on the cabin was progressing well. Dave was absent for a few days due to finishing a project he and Stan had been working on that they were eager to finish. He was looking forward to getting back to joining the others in completing the cabin. It was a satisfying job to be working with people he had known for many years, who had also taught him a great deal. He was lucky: a lovely wife and home, a good partner and great friends, plus people he admired and respected. What more could a man need? He whistled as he worked, content with his life but unaware of the event happening close by.

Simon, Abe and Stan had just fitted the roof to the cabin when Jeannie came flying out of the kitchen door shouting at them to get indoors quickly. She rushed back in followed closely by the three men, who were all frowning and wondering what could be wrong.

Felicity was standing by the telephone, looking at it as though she wasn't sure what it was. Her face was ashen and tears were streaming down her cheeks.

Simon rushed to her and she fell against him, now crying openly.

"What is it, Felicity? What's happened? Are the children OK?" he asked.

Abe had his arms around Jeannie; she too was crying. "Where are the children?" Abe asked gently, "Are they OK?" He held her away from him and looked directly at her, shaking her a little to gain her attention.

"It's Pops," she said. "He's dead, and James saw it all." She sagged suddenly, and Abe caught her quickly before she fell to the ground.

He picked her up, laid her on the sofa and then turned to Simon. "You go Simon; go to James. I'll see to these two."

He looked at his watch. The twins wouldn't need fetching from playschool for a while, Janine was at school, and Myles must be asleep as he wasn't in the room. Quietly, he asked Jeannie where James was, then went to Simon and gently took Felicity from him. "Go, Simon; go to James. He's in Ray's apartment."

Simon left, knowing that the two women would be well cared for – Abe was very capable and could even manage the baby if necessary.

Stan, rooted to the spot, listened to everything being said; he was shocked to the core. He realised quickly that he would be in the way, so his help wasn't needed at the moment. He left unobtrusively, went out to the cabin and tidied the tools away, knowing no more work would be done today. He left a note for Abe and Simon, left immediately and, before long, found himself outside the door to Bella and Seb's annexe.

He knocked on the door, hoping that Bella would be home. The smile on her face as she opened the door told Stan how pleased she was to see him. As he stepped inside, the smile on her face died.

"What's wrong? What's happened?" she questioned.

He hugged her to him, but there was no way to soften the blow. "It's Pops," he said, "He's died from a heart attack."

He held Bella close to him as she cried openly, not wanting to believe the awful news. When she stopped shaking, he led her quietly to the living room, settled her gently on the sofa and went into the kitchen to make some tea.

A short while later, he returned and handed her a cup of tea.

Bella looked up at Stan, took hold of his hand and pulled him down to sit next to her. "Stay with me please. I'm so glad you came here to tell me. I need you with me." She leant against him, still holding his hand, heartbroken at the news of Pops, but contented to have the man she loved by her side.

The door to the annexe crashed open, and Seb stood in the doorway. "Is it true?" he blurted out, his face white with shock. "Has Pops really died?"

Stan hardly had time to respond to his question before Seb rushed out again, calling over his shoulder, "I'm going to find Mum and Dad!"

It had only taken Simon a few minutes to get to Ray's

apartment. He flew up the steps, and as the door was open, he entered and found his son staring out of the window in the lounge, not moving.

"James," Simon said quietly and calmly, "tell me what happened."

James sighed heavily and turned to face his Dad, wincing as he moved, his face pale and a huge bruise forming on his cheek.

"Good God son, what on earth happened?" Simon went to help James, sat him down and waited for him to speak.

"I rang the bell, and Pops opened it, then he went to go up the stairs. He fell backwards from about halfway up, and as I was behind him, he knocked me down as he fell. I hit my face on the stair post as he landed on me and I fell against the open door. My ribs hurt and my leg is grazed from the doorstep." He stopped speaking.

Simon noticed how James was struggling to breathe. "Where's Ray now?"

"I called for an ambulance, Dad, but he was dead when they got here. I only just managed to lift him off me so I could use the phone upstairs. I tried to help him, but he didn't move and wasn't breathing. He was just lying there. It was awful, Dad; I couldn't help him." Hysteria was rising in James's voice and his eyes filled with tears.

Simon put his arms around James as he started sobbing, shock and pain causing him to shake with the realisation of what had occurred.

"May I come up?" a voice called from the bottom of the stairs. "I'm a paramedic, and I've come back to check if the young man who was here with Mr Luxton is OK."

"Come up," Simon replied, "He needs some attention."

Half an hour later, James was lying on the sofa, quieter and almost asleep after the paramedic had sedated him to ease his pain and shock. The paramedic explained to Simon that the ambulance crew had called for him to attend James as they left to take Ray to the hospital in Plymouth. James had assured them he'd be OK, as he wasn't badly hurt, and that he'd called his Mum after he'd called for the ambulance. The paramedic confirmed to Simon that Mr Luxton was dead, probably from a heart attack. He asked if Simon knew who his next of kin was as they would need to make contact with them.

"I assume his sister, the landlady at The Tavern must be," Simon replied.

He turned to look at James, who was now asleep and breathing easier. His cheek had now turned purple, and his eye was swollen and turning black. The graze on his leg had been dressed, and Simon had some morphine pills to give to James later that day. The paramedic left to go to see Lucy.

Simon then had time to think about what had happened. He felt tears trickling down his cheeks and was suddenly aware of the deep sadness he felt at the loss of this man who had been like a father to him, who had played such a huge part in their lives, and whose death would leave an enormous gap in the lives of all of them.

His thoughts then turned to Felicity; this would be a huge shock to her. Ray had been such an important person in her life. He put his head in his hands and sobbed openly at the unfairness of life and why such a good man should have been taken from them.

Chapter Twelve

Felicity was distraught; she felt the loss of Ray so deeply he'd been like a father to her. She couldn't remember feeling this way for a long time, not since her own father had died when she was sixteen. The twins couldn't understand, they were fractious and grizzly, wanting to know where Pops had gone and why he didn't come to see them. She fed Myles as though on automatic pilot; even *he* cried and was fretful. James shut himself in his half-finished cabin, refusing to come out even for meals.

Simon too was devastated at the loss of his greatest friend; he had no time to grieve as he was trying to comfort the whole family. He worried for them all, especially Felicity, as she turned away from him every time he'd tried to console her. Anger and resentment built up inside him, which had transmitted to the children. He raised his voice and shouted at the twins, something he had never done before. Surprised at this unknown side to their father, they both burst into tears and ran outside. Horrified with himself, Simon suddenly felt dreadful; then immediately felt ashamed and contrite. This situation had to be resolved; he would make Felicity face up to the fact that Ray had gone. First, though, he must find the twins.

He knew Felicity was upstairs in her sitting room, feeding Myles, so he went outside and saw the twins at the door of James's cabin.

They were trying to peer in through the windows on the door and shouting, "*James, James, wake up!*" They turned as Simon approached, and Cassie said "Daddy, Daddy, James isn't in. He's gone!"

Sensing something was wrong, Simon shooed the girls out of the way and knocked on the door, shouting for James. Although he hadn't emerged from the cabin, James had always answered with an abrupt, "Go away." This time, though, there was no answer. Simon walked quickly round the cabin, looking through the windows, but no one was to be seen.

He rushed back to the house, grabbed the spare key, went back to the cabin, told the twins to wait outside for him and then opened the door. It was deserted; the bed hadn't been slept in. It looked almost as though James had never been there. The colour drained from his face; they'd been so wrapped up in their own feelings they'd forgotten it was James who had been with Ray when he died.

He turned around, scooped up the twins and dashed back indoors. Once inside, he put them down, told them to go and play in their room, then picked up the phone and dialled Abe and Jeannie's number.

"Abe, can you get over here quickly, please? Bring Jeannie and the children with you; we need help!" Simon crashed the phone back on its cradle and went upstairs to find Felicity.

He opened the door to her sitting room. She looked lovely, and his heart lurched. For a moment, he stood in the doorway, how he loved this woman: she was his life, his soul and everything to him. After taking a deep breath to calm his feelings, he stepped inside the room and went across to her. She smiled up at him, and his heart lurched again. He didn't smile in return and his expression transmitted to her that something was wrong. She sat up clutching Myles closely to her.

Before he could say anything, Jeannie called from the hallway, "Simon, Felicity, what's going on?"

Felicity stood up, her voice trembling as she asked, "What is it, Simon? What's happened?"

"James has gone," Simon replied.

Chapter Thirteen

Simon rushed forward as Felicity crumpled; he grabbed Myles from her and yelled to Jeannie to come up quickly.

"Simon, where are you?" Jeannie's voice was bordering on panic.

"In the sitting room Jeannie; come and get Myles, please."

Jeannie quickly came in as requested and took Myles from Simon, her eyebrows raised questioningly as she took in the scene. Felicity was on the floor, stirring and trying to sit up; Simon was by her side, helping her and whispering to her. He picked her up in his arms and gestured to Jeannie to go downstairs.

Instinct took over, and once in the kitchen, Jeannie handed Myles to Abe, gave each of the children biscuits and ushered them into the twins' room, telling them to play until she came to fetch them.

Meanwhile, back in the kitchen, Myles was asleep on Abe's shoulder, and Simon was settling Felicity into the rocking chair.

Calmly and softly, Abe enquired, "What's happened, Simon?"

Holding on to Felicity's hand, his voice trembling with a mix of emotions, Simon explained that James seemed to have disappeared, but when and to where he had no idea.

"We've been so entrenched in our own feelings about Ray that we forgot our sixteen-year-old son has received a tremendous shock. It's our fault he's gone. "His voice broke, he turned away, angry at himself and Felicity for not realising how James must be feeling.

Jeannie stopped her process of tea-making and, with tears running down her face, looked at Abe. "We're all at fault; one of us should have realised."

Abe stood up, shifting Myles to his other shoulder indicating that he would take the baby upstairs to his cot, and then they could discuss what to do next when Abe came back down. He was so calm and collected that the atmosphere in the kitchen had changed, being calmer and quieter.

Abe returned smiling at Felicity. "Myles is fast asleep; he'll be fine for quite a while. I have some ideas about James, I don't think he'll be far away. He most likely needed time to himself away from everyone. He's very young, but he's sensible and perceptive. He has probably gone because he couldn't face up to being mollycoddled by us all. Which, let's face it, we would have done – all of us. Let's give him his space so he can work it out for himself. When he needs help – if he needs help – he'll ask for it. He's very much like you in that regard, Simon."

Abe paused, and Simon looked hard at him knowing that he was right and realising his perception of James was accurate. He paced around the kitchen, unaware of the others, as he considered what they could do. Although he knew in his heart that Abe was right, he had an urgent need to search for his son.

Abe sensed this and quietly asked when they'd last seen him. As the minutes went by, Jeannie busied herself with tea and biscuits. Felicity furrowed her brow, trying to remember, while Simon went to the window, also trying to recall when they last saw James.

"Mummy, when can we have lunch? Why are Uncle Abe and Auntie Jeannie here? Can Janine have lunch with us? And why is everyone so sad?" Katie had erupted into the kitchen, closely followed by Cassie and Janine, all clamouring together to have lunch, with Janine stating firmly that she was going to stay with Cassie and Katie.

The interruption from the children lightened the mood; the adults all smiled at their exuberance, as they were now climbing all over Abe and demanding he be a horse, "Just like Pops."

Pandemonium ensued, including a bellowing wail from Myles, who had obviously woken up and was hungry. A sense of normality settled on the assembled group, and half an hour later saw the adults sitting at the table with cheese and biscuits, the children on the floor mat with sandwiches and crisps, and Myles gurgling alongside them, also content having now been fed.

With her eyes lighting up with excitement, Jeannie suddenly said, "Will James have his mobile with him?

Surely he'll have taken it with him! Why don't you send him a message? I'm sure he would reply to let you know he's OK!"

They all looked at Jeannie, surprise on their faces. Why hadn't they thought of that before?

Simon stood up and dashed out of the door. A few moments later, he was back. "I can't see his mobile anywhere, so he must have it with him. Where's yours, Felicity? We'll send him a text."

Before she could reply, Simon had gone from the room and returned with Felicity's handbag. With trembling fingers, she retrieved her mobile from her bag and sent a short message to their son, simply asking for him to please let them know he was OK and to come home when he was ready ending her message "with love from Mum and Dad".

She stood up going across to Simon and cuddled up to him saying "Thank you, all of you; Ray wouldn't have wanted us to wallow in misery. I'm sure I've been too selfish in my grief. I'm also sure James will be OK, but we must now help Lucy and Michael. They'll have an enormous amount to deal with, what with sorting out the funeral and Ray's affairs."

Simon gathered Felicity tightly into his arms, not wanting to let her go, even though she wriggled to get away as their youngest son was being encouraged to try crisps by his sisters!

"Mummy can I stay with Katie, Cassie and Myles until bedtime?" Janine's plaintive question broke the moment.

They all laughed and decided they would all stay

together, have a buffet dinner, and discuss the best way they could help Lucy and Michael. Simon went off to see if they would both like to come along and spend the afternoon with the rest of them, as the pub had been shut until after Ray's funeral.

He came back with Lucy and Michael, and together they spent the afternoon arranging Ray's funeral. In the backs of their minds, all of them were listening out for the mobile to ping – hopefully, with a message from James.

Chapter Fourteen

James got up from his desk, his heart heavy; he was exhausted. He'd hidden away in the cabin, not being able to face his family and friends knowing they would try to comfort him. He didn't want that. He had to work it through for himself. He was tired, dog tired, of telling people to go away when all he wanted was peace.

With sudden clarity of thought, he grabbed his jacket, picked up his phone and wallet, opened the cabin door and went out. Quietly, he locked the cabin and crept around the garden; the house was in darkness as it was late, and he presumed that everyone would be asleep. He went through the gate and into the lane, making his way towards Ray's apartment. He knew where Ray hid the spare key, having used it before at Ray's invitation. His heart was thumping; he just hoped and prayed that no one had taken it. Relief flooded through him when the key was exactly where he remembered, so he took it and let himself in.

The apartment was in total darkness, but he knew his way around. He went through to the kitchen, got himself a glass of water, and then went and sat at the top of the stairs. How long he was there, he didn't know; he just wanted to be there to try to ease the shock of Ray's plunge down the stairs and his own fall following Ray landing on top of him.

Sometime later the light was beginning to show through the windows, and James knew he must go before the owners of the Estate Agency beneath the apartment arrived to open up the office.

Stiff and cold from sitting all night, James struggled to his feet, his cracked ribs and bruised leg now painful and aching. He put the glass back in the kitchen and painfully hobbled down the stairs. Carefully, he let himself out, locked the door and placed the key back in its hiding place.

What now? Where should he go? He felt tears welling in his eyes; he was close to breaking down and needed someone to be wise; to share his sorrow, but whom? Who could give him what he needed? Aware that he didn't want to be found at the flat, he moved away and walked out of the village, away from people, houses and noise.

He walked until his chest was too painful to move further. He didn't know where he was, but it was somewhere out in the country. He'd unconsciously chosen the smallest lanes to walk down.

He sat down with his back against a tree, as tears trickled down his cheeks once more, but he felt a certain strength from the solidity of the tree he was leaning against.

Time passed; he dozed and then woke up fully to realise he was thirsty and hungry. It was now late afternoon, and he had been sitting there all day. Stretching his arms and legs, he stood up, sore and very stiff. He was calmer now, more at peace, but he was still on the edge of breaking down. He looked around him and tried to get his bearings; he must make his way back, not home, but he knew where he wanted to go. They would help him; he knew that with absolute certainty. He moved away from the tree and walked back along the lane he had come down.

Several times, he came to a junction, but he continued, an innate sense of direction keeping him on the right path. It was approaching 6pm when he finally saw a signpost that confirmed where he was. He stopped and leant against the sign, as he was so tired and just wanted to sleep.

Should I call them first? he wondered. He got his phone out, turned it on and found the text message from his parents. He suddenly felt guilty; he'd forgotten all about them and the fact that they would be so worried. Now he knew what he would do.

He headed off back towards Little Trenchard. He would get his friends to phone his parents when he got there, as he couldn't face them himself; he needed more time – one last effort to make sense of what had happened and his own feelings afterwards.

It was nearly 8pm when he arrived and rang the doorbell.

Chapter Fifteen

Bella was just pouring water into her teacup when the doorbell rang; she was still in her uniform having only just got home from her shift at the hospital.

"Seb, will you answer that, please?" she shouted to her brother.

With a sigh, he ran down the stairs from his room, opened the door and caught James as he fell into the hallway.

"Bella, get yourself down here quick; it's James."

Bella immediately reacted to the urgency in Seb's voice. She ran downstairs to find her brother kneeling at the side of a comatose James. He was pale and shivering, unconscious but not deeply so.

Bella's nursing training took over. "Get me blankets, a pillow, some water and a drop of brandy from Mum and Dad. No, cancel that; leave that till later. Don't let Mum and Dad know yet that he's here."

Seb rushed off, leaving James in Bella's capable hands. By the time he got back, James was stirring,

Bella had taken his pulse and got him into the recovery position. Rapidly, she took the pillow and blankets from Seb, then wrapped James up in the blanket to warm him. With the pillow supporting his head, she held the glass gently to his lips. Seb had thought to bring a straw (he'd obviously learnt something from his sister).

Within a few minutes, James was conscious, groaning from the pain in his chest and leg.

"Don't say anything, James. We'll get you upstairs to bed as soon as you can stand up."

Within a few minutes, supporting James between them, he was in Bella's bed, now comfortable and warm. He looked at Bella and Seb, who were both sitting on the bed either side of him. James looked at them both and said "Bella…..I….." he then burst into tears, with wracking great sobs.

Seb was astounded.

Bella looked at her brother and told him, "Go, Seb; go and phone Felicity and Simon. Tell them James is here and we'll bring him home as soon as he's awake – just that, no more. Then tell Mum and Dad too, but don't let them come in to see James. Tell Mum I'll talk to her later."

Seb went off, glad to be away from the charged emotion of James's sobs. Bella held James's hand and then drew him to her, putting her arms around him to give him the comfort he obviously needed. He was like a brother to her; a few years younger, but they had grown up together and were very close.

If only… she thought, if only this were Stan in my arms.

Finally, James fell asleep. Bella gently laid him back down on her bed and covered him up to keep him warm and cosy. She'd just got him settled when Seb came back into the room.

"Simon and Felicity are so relieved to know James is OK. I told them all we'll take him home as soon as he's ready to go. Mum and Dad know too; apparently, they've all been together today, including Lucy and Michael, and have been discussing the arrangements for Pops' funeral." He broke off and looked at his sister questioningly. "Is everything OK, Sis? You look different somehow."

Bella smiled at Seb. "I'm fine. I'll just stay with James a while to make sure he's OK, but I'm fine; everything's OK."

Seb shrugged his shoulders; he really didn't understand the way women think.

*

The following morning, James woke feeling more settled, more in control of himself and strangely comforted. The room was empty; Bella was nowhere to be seen. He heard someone moving around, got out of bed and opened the door just as Seb emerged from his room.

"Hi James," he said in greeting, "You look so much better this morning. You can use my bathroom to freshen up, if you'd like? It's more manly than Bella's! Help yourself to whatever you need. Bella is downstairs making breakfast, so join us as soon as you're ready."

Seb ran off down the stairs, and James took his advice to freshen up before joining them.

He was so pleased he'd decided to come to Bella and Seb's place. It was exactly what he had needed: comfort and peace, given quietly without questions or interrogation. As he settled down to toast and cereal, he realised for the first time in days, he was hungry.

"See you later," Seb called as he rushed off to get the bus to college; he was happy to see his friend looking so much better.

Bella asked James if he wanted more coffee, then she sat down and waited for James to speak.

"Won't your parents think it strange that I stayed here last night?" he asked Bella.

"No, they won't," she answered him. "We've been friends for years, having grown up together, so who else could you turn to?" Bella stopped as she saw the hurt look on James's face, and as tears gathered in his eyes, she placed her hand over his. "Remember, James, we all had the great privilege of knowing Ray, so in his own way, he's left us all with a special gift. How lucky we all are."

"Thanks, Bella; that means a great deal, and thanks for last night too."

Bella got up from the table, gathering up the remains from breakfast, then tidied the small kitchen. Once she'd finished, she stated, "Come on James, let's get you home."

Chapter Sixteen

James and Bella walked slowly towards Simon's Fel, both subdued from their own thoughts.

Unexpectedly, Bella said, "James, I want to tell you something I haven't told anyone else: I am going to marry Stan – soon, I hope. I think he now knows how I feel, and I want you to know."

James stopped walking, stunned by what Bella had said.

Hurriedly, Bella took hold of James's arm. "Keep it to yourself for now, please." She then gave him a peck on the cheek as she put her arm through his. She had a smile on her face for the rest of the way.

Still stunned but moved by her trust in him, James straightened his shoulders and prepared himself to greet his parents after his abrupt disappearance.

When they arrived, Bella popped in to say hello to Simon and Felicity, then she left them alone; she was sure they needed the time together.

James made his apologies to his parents for the

worry he'd caused, but he made it clear to them that he wasn't ready to discuss it all with them yet. He needed time, but he would talk to them when he was ready. He went straight off to his room, not wanting to be with anyone.

*

Life at Simon's Fel became more strained as the days went by. Felicity was more distraught each day as Ray's funeral approached. Simon was being pulled in all directions by the whole family, and not knowing which way to turn, he finally realised that things couldn't carry on the way they were and they all needed a break. Firstly, he visited Lucy at the pub and arranged for Felicity and Myles to stay there for a few days, then he arranged for the twins to stay with Jeannie and Abe. James would stay with Simon; they needed time alone together.

No one argued with Simon about his plans. The twins went off happily with Jeannie and Abe, knowing that they would have a great time playing with Janine. Felicity calmly went off to The Tavern; being with Lucy would be all the comfort she needed. She also was very aware that Simon and James needed time alone together.

Simon worked hard over the next few days to complete all the work required to finish the cabin. Then James cleared his room in the house and moved all his belongings over to the cabin. Nothing much was discussed between them, but a better understanding had been reached. They were now content in each other's company. They finished the final touches to the cabin between them, and James had moved in completely. He was now the proud resident of his own "home", having moved out of the house to spend his first night alone.

Simon had seen the children every day and went to stay with Felicity each night. Tonight, he could give her the news that James had moved into the cabin, and tomorrow, he would start moving the twins' belongings into their new, bigger room.

*

Simon went into Felicity's room at The Tavern, smiling and excited about James's move. The smile died on his face when he saw how despondent Felicity was looking, and Myles was being irritable. As Simon tried to comfort her, she turned away from him once again, rejecting his efforts. He just lost his temper with her and stormed out of the room; ran straight into Lucy, who was on her way up the stairs, knocking her sideways; and carried on out of The Tavern door.

Astounded, Lucy sat down on the stairs, burst into tears and sobbed. Her brother was dead, her best friends were seemingly growing apart, and then there was Michael and Justin, who were just wandering about not knowing what to do! Why was life so difficult?

Felicity heard Lucy; it broke through her own sorrow, and she went swiftly out of her room and hugged Lucy to her. They cried together, the relief for both of them causing different reactions. Felicity woke up to her own selfishness, realising just how much she'd neglected her own family. Lucy gave way to her inner feelings and let out all the anguish and despair she'd been feeling since Ray had died. Suddenly, they both smiled at each other, the tension and relief dissolved by their tears.

Felicity stood up. "I must go home. I need to see Simon, James and the twins." She rushed off, picked up Myles from his cot and dashed out of the pub.

Chapter Seventeen

Lucy stood up and went shakily downstairs to find Michael and Justin. They were sitting at the table, not talking, with both of them looking lost and forlorn.

"Michael," Lucy said, a smile on her face, "I..."She got no further.

Michael jumped up and gathered her in his arms Knowing her so well, he realised she'd come to terms with Ray's death.

Justin came over, put his arms round both his parents briefly, then went out, stating that he was going to meet up with friends. He needed to be alone now. His Mum and Dad were OK, and he just needed to be by himself to adjust to the situation. He missed his uncle; he'd been a good counsellor when Justin needed help, and sometimes parents were too close. Uncle Ray's advice had been good and solid; Justin would now take that advice and put into practice the plans he'd considered. Uncle Ray had been a good man.

Justin had worked in London for a long time, and although he was settled in a good job, something was missing. He was unsettled in himself, and the death of his uncle had enhanced his unsettlement. He'd done well at University, but for the past few years, nothing had ever seemed right for him. He went to visit his parents often. Also, he could never find anyone he wanted to spend his life with. His parents were happy and contented with each other, but no one he'd met so far could match their happiness. He knew he should change his way of life, and Uncle Ray's death had given him the push he needed. He would finalise the plans he was devising and turn them into a new life for himself away from England!

*

Felicity hurried home from The Tavern, she rushed indoors, looking for Simon. She found him in her sitting room. He looked so dejected, his head in his hands and just sitting on the floor. He must have heard her come in as he jerked his head round in her direction, then stood up slowly. He stayed still, just watching her. She then walked towards him with Myles in her arms. The smile on her face was beautiful, her eyes full of love. He gently took both of them in his arms and kissed her passionately, his own eyes gleaming intensely with those unique silver specks.

*

By the end of the day, Simon and Felicity had collected the twins and all their things from Abe and Jeannie's, plus all the bits and pieces from The Tavern that Felicity had left there. Felicity wanted to see James in the cabin, but Simon stopped her, telling her that James would come over later when he was ready. The twins ran around James's old room, already planning where they wanted their new beds to go.

Lucy and Michael put together the final plans for Ray's funeral, which would take place the next day.

*

James, meanwhile, spent the rest of the day sketching. He worked his way through a whole sketchbook, drawing whatever came into his mind. When he'd finished, he put the book away without looking at what he'd drawn. Tomorrow, after Ray's funeral, he would tell his Mum what he was going to do; he knew his Dad would back him up, albeit reluctantly. Against all his instincts, Simon had given his consent. James was going to London; he'd secured a work placement at the law firm that Simon's father had started.

James checked his watch, the twins would be in bed, so he would go across to the house now to visit his parents.

Chapter Eighteen

Although it was a sad day, the weather for Ray's funeral was warm and dry. Most of the villagers had been at the Church; Ray had been such an important part of everyone's life, and they wanted Lucy and Michael to know how much he'd been loved by them all.

The Tavern was full to bursting, as Michael and Lucy had invited everyone who attended the funeral to join the family at "Ray's party" after the service. There had been many tears and much sorrow, but laughter too and so many happy memories. Finally, towards the end of the "party" there was just the family and a few very close friends left at The Tavern.

Michael called for silence announcing that he had some important things to say. He cleared his throat, took a large file that had been lying on the corner of the bar and began, "I expect you're all aware that Lucy, as Ray's sister, is his next of kin. Some months ago, Ray asked me to be the Executor of his Will. I must confess to being somewhat surprised, but honoured, nevertheless. It has been left to me to read his Will; I think everyone who's a beneficiary is here."

He turned to face Lucy and smiled happily at her. "Ray has left you all the contents of his flat and also the flat itself. You can sell it or keep it, whatever you wish. It has legally been registered as a separate dwelling from the Estate Agency. Mr and Mrs Carlyon signed it over to Ray two months ago."

Lucy gasped at this unexpected gift from her brother, and tears of happiness and gratitude filled her eyes.

Michael continued, "To all his '"Grandchildren"', namely James, Katie, Cassie and Myles Grantley; Sebastian, Bella and Janine Bresland –he's left £5,000 each. To my nephew Justin, he's given the sum of £10,000, with a request for him to follow his dreams."

Michael paused to take a drink, and he cast his eyes around the room. Shock and surprise were reflected in the expressions of everyone there; the younger ones weren't sure what was happening, and the others were astounded at Ray's generosity.

Once again, Michael began to speak: "I have great pleasure in announcing two special bequests: the remainder of Ray's estate is divided equally between Simon and Felicity Grantley, and Abe and Jeannie Bresland. The amount to be announced when all other bequests are paid and probate has been granted. As the Executor, I'm very happy to say that the sums you'll receive are likely to be considerable."

Michael sat down, relieved to have done his duty, happy for Lucy and thrilled for Justin; he was amazed too that Ray had been so generous to them all. He smiled across at Lucy; they would have much to talk about later. But in the meantime, he would get up and open some champagne so they could all toast Ray.

Felicity was in total shock; she sat holding onto Simon's arm, not believing what she'd just heard. She looked across at Jeannie and saw the same expression on her friend's face. Neither Simon nor Abe could think of anything to say.

Michael broke the spell by handing a glass of champagne to each of the adults.

As one, they all stood up and, following Michael's lead, they simply said, "To Ray."

Chapter Nineteen

It took a few weeks for the members of Ray's family to come to terms with the fortuitous effect his Will had left them in.

Justin had immediately announced plans that he was emigrating to New Zealand. He was so adamant about this decision that he gave in his notice at work and put his flat in London on the market, including everything in it except the personal items he wished to keep. He moved back to Little Trenchard with just his car, his clothes and his personal things. He spent all his time sorting out visas, researching jobs and the area he most wanted to live in. He had settled on Auckland; it appealed to him, and several jobs there interested him. Michael and Lucy didn't try to dissuade him as they were so pleased that, after such a long time, he finally knew what he wanted to do. They would miss him so much, but they could always visit!

James, Seb and Bella all immediately opened savings accounts in which to keep their unexpected windfalls for the future. The younger children had savings accounts opened for them by their respective parents where the money would remain until they were old enough to decide for themselves what they wished to do.

Lucy and Michael decided to rent out the flat to earn an income and maybe move into it whenever they decided to retire.

Simon, Felicity, Abe and Jeannie sensibly decided to wait until after the probate had been settled; until then they each hadn't any idea exactly how much their inheritance would amount to.

Simon still had one important thing on his mind: James and his choice of career. What should or could he do? It worried him constantly, but he kept his own counsel; he wouldn't mention it until James did.

The children were all growing up, each one of them developing their own individual personalities: the twins were due to start school soon, Myles was fast approaching going to playschool, Janine wanted to study art and needlework, and James was still set on becoming a lawyer.

Three things happened on the same day that affected all of them.

Bella came home with Stan, both of them so happy and excited. They announced they were getting married the following week – next Saturday to be exact. They had it all planned, Dave would be the best man and

Janine would be Bella's bridesmaid. They were looking for somewhere to live.

James had confirmed his intention to study law, had secured a University place in Bristol and would definitely be taking up the offer of a work placement to advance his chosen career. He was studying very hard to achieve the required grades at university.

Sebastian decided to quit college; he was going to New Zealand with Justin and wanted to work on a sheep station. He'd already arranged the necessary visas (with Justin's help) and was ready to go as soon as they could book their flights.

Uproar ensued!

By mutual consent, they all met at The Tavern the next day; Michael and Lucy had agreed that they could all meet there as it involved each of them. They decided to shut the pub and just put a notice on the door stating "CLOSED TODAY DUE TO UNFORESEEN CIRCUMSTANCES – OPEN TOMORROW AS USUAL".

When the adults were all assembled, with the youngsters all at school, Abe addressed them all: "Let's start with our surprising news. As Stan and Bella are here, maybe they'll explain?"

Stan rose to his feet, with Bella standing beside him. "We want to be married, and soon. There's nothing to wait for; I have savings, and we can easily find somewhere to live. I have a good job, a good partner, an excellent mentor (he stopped there and smiled at Abe) who's soon to be my father-in-law. A bit late, I know, as we've already made the announcement, but I do hope you'll give us your blessing, Abe. You too, Mrs Abe."

Abe jumped up immediately, grabbed hold of Jeannie, then went to Stan and Bella, beaming at them. "We're delighted for you both."

It took some time for the hubbub to quieten down; there were so many questions to ask and answer. The consensus of opinion agreed upon would be that Abe, Jeannie, Stan and Bella would meet the next day to make all the plans.

Justin stood up next and explained to his parents that he'd reached a crossroads in his life and needed a new direction; it was as simple as that. He would miss everyone, but he was his own man, knew what he now needed and felt that New Zealand could offer that to him. Facing Abe and Jeannie, he said, "It was Seb's idea to come with me. *He* asked *me*; I didn't in any way influence him. He's so sure and mature for his age, with a great determination to succeed. I do hope you'll give your permission, but if you don't, I shall still be going." He sat down.

Everyone was silent for a few moments, and then Michael stood up again. "We knew Justin was unsettled, so we aren't surprised he wants to emigrate. We'll miss him tremendously. I *am* surprised Seb wants to go, but I know he'll have a good friend in Justin."

Everyone turned in Seb's direction.

He was sitting with his parents, who were watching

him closely, puzzling as to what he would do. He looked directly and questioningly at his parents. "Will you let me go, Mum? Dad? I've been thinking hard as to what I really want to do. I promise I'll continue to study accountancy while I'm away, and I *will* come back!"

Abe and Jeannie both hugged him, knowing they couldn't refuse their very grown up young son.

Michael called for silence and decided they could all do with something to eat and drink Lucy, Felicity, Jeannie and Bella went to prepare some food, while Stan and Abe chatted about the upcoming wedding and where they could possibly live. Justin and Seb joined the discussion, assuring everyone that they would definitely be around for the wedding. Only Simon and James were quiet, each with their own thoughts occupying their minds.

Just as the food was being brought out, Simon rose and gestured to James to follow him, which he did. As they stepped outside, Simon put his hand on James's shoulder and told him earnestly but gently, "I will always support you in whatever you choose to do. Just promise me you will always be honest, truthful and sincere." He smiled at James.

"Thanks, Dad; I will," James confirmed.

They both went back into the pub. James looked across the room and smiled widely at his Mum, with thumbs raised.

Felicity smiled back at him, relieved and happy. As James walked past her, she was astonished to notice silver specks shining in his eyes.

Chapter Twenty

The next week was taken up by all of them arranging plans for Bella and Stan's wedding. They'd already arranged a licence, booked the Registry Office and had decided they would spend a few days at Marazion in Cornwall.

All the women went shopping in Exeter to find something special to wear, including Janine, who had permission to take the day off school! She was so excited to be Bella's bridesmaid and to have her own special dress. Their day of shopping was exhausting, but very successful. They'd left Abe in charge of the young ones, as he was so very capable and able to cope on his own. Everyone happily went their own way back to their own homes, content after their day out.

Michael looked round at Lucy when their customers were all settled and their barmaid was calmly tending to a couple at the bar. "Come upstairs, Lucy; I have an idea I want to discuss with you. It's quiet at the moment so we can leave Sandra for a while, and we won't be long." He took Lucy's arm, smiled at Sandra, and guided Lucy upstairs.

He explained his idea to Lucy straight away, getting more excited as he did. "I think it's a plan that would be a perfect solution for everyone!" He stopped talking and handed Lucy a glass of wine, which he'd poured out while detailing his idea. He was beaming.

Lucy was stunned, pleased and wondering why she hadn't thought of it herself. So much had happened recently that she'd had no time to think about Ray's flat. She smiled joyfully as Michael sat down alongside her, waiting for her reaction. "What a great idea! It's perfect. All we need now is for Bella and Stan to agree!"

Michael rushed down to the bar and spoke urgently to Sandra to see if she would mind if they went out for about an hour; however, if she got really busy, Justin would step in and help her as he was still living with his parents until he left for New Zealand.

A short while later, Michael and Lucy walked to Abe and Jeannie's house and knocked on the door to the extension.

Bella opened it, surprised to see Lucy and Michael, "Come in, please," she said, leading the way into the living room.

Stan was there and looked questioningly at their unexpected guests. He jumped up and asked if he could get them a drink, but Lucy and Michael declined as they just wanted to convey their idea to Stan and Bella.

"We wanted to offer you both the chance to rent Ray's flat; that is, if you would like to," Michael said, "We would be so happy to have you as our tenants."

Stan and Bella looked astounded. No one spoke for a moment, and Lucy held her breath, waiting for their answer. Bella and Stan looked at each other, not quite believing what they had just heard. Stan jumped up, shook Michael's hand, kissed Lucy on the cheek and then embraced Bella picking her up and swinging her around.

"I think that means yes," laughed Lucy.

Bella rushed from the room and went through to find her parents. Moments later, they came in, surprised to see Lucy and Michael there. Excitedly, Bella and Stan told them of the news about Ray's flat. Amazed, Abe and Jeannie, caught up in the air of unbelievable joy, hugged and shook hands with everyone. When they were all calm, they sat down, still in a joyous mood, Abe happily going next door to find drinks to celebrate.

As there would be paperwork to organise, it was decided that Abe and Michael would take charge of that while Jeannie and Lucy would clear Ray's flat of all his personal things and prepare it for Stan and Bella to move in.

*

The level of excitement continued to engulf them all over the coming days, and the day of the wedding was suddenly upon them. It was a beautiful day. They had a small, simple ceremony and then everyone gathered together at Abe and Jeannie's house for a buffet wedding tea. Bella looked stunning in her gorgeous-but-simple cream dress, the smile on her face glowing radiantly. Stan looked so proud; he still wasn't quite believing how he'd managed to become a member of this wonderful family. It was a happy day for everyone, even James, who hadn't yet quite come to terms with Pops' death, but was somehow comforted knowing that Bella and Stan would be living in the flat.

Things were beginning to settle. James put his shoulders back, feeling suddenly that he'd grown and was finding a new side to himself. He looked around the assembled group, caught his father gazing at him, and he smiled in return – both of them realising that they'd reached a new understanding.

Chapter Twenty-One

Michael and Lucy wanted to get Ray's flat ready for Bella and Stan to move into on their return from Cornwall. They persuaded Justin to take over the running of the pub for them, whilst Sandra agreed to run the bar on a full-time basis for the week, with Justin's help for the heavy work. They already had cleaning staff to take care of the bed and breakfast rooms, so it just required engaging a temporary chef, which was quite easily sorted through a local Temporary Recruitment Agency they'd previously used frequently.

That done, Michael and Abe decided between them that they would paint the whole flat and clean all the carpets. Lucy and Jeannie would take care of cleaning the cupboards and furniture, plus clearing out all Ray's possessions, which they would store at The Tavern to sort through later.

Simon was tasked with doing the school runs, and Felicity washed and ironed bedding, curtains, towels and cushion covers. They all worked hard, each with their own thoughts, which culminated in the many changes to their lives.

Primarily, though, their goal was to make sure everything was ready for Bella and Stan's return.

Back at the pub, Lucy and Michael prepared a special lunch for the newlywed's homecoming, with all the families invited, including Dave and his wife Vanessa. The excitement was mounting; there were gifts from everyone, and even the children had contributed!

Suddenly, the door opened – Bella and Stan had arrived. They were overwhelmed to see everyone there, and what were all those parcels on the table?

It took a while for all the greetings to be completed and the drinks distributed, but at last, silence ensued.

Stan cleared his throat to say simply, "Thank you, everyone. This has been such a surprise, and Bella and I can't think of a better homecoming."

Everyone joined in with toasting the happy couple, more drinks were ordered, and finally, after the excellent buffet lunch, the gifts were opened.

Bella and Stan were thrilled to find the parcels included starter packs of tins, packages and jars of all types of food. There were new towels and bedding, plus useful and necessary items that would be needed, including a kettle, toaster, iron and ironing board! Saucepans and a set of crockery were also among the gifts. In fact, there was enough for any young couple setting up a new home. Bella was crying happy tears and Stan just looked bewildered.

At this point, Michael beckoned Lucy, and a few moments later, they left to take Bella and Stan to their new home.

Everyone left at the party helped to clear up, including tidying the gifts into the corner of the room to be transported to the flat the next day. They washed up and put the furniture back to rights. Justin and Sandra heaved a sigh of relief that their brief tenure as "Landlord" and "Landlady" was over!

Michael and Lucy returned to The Tavern sometime later and happily reported that all their hard work at Ray's flat had thrilled and astonished Bella and Stan. They were so happy with what had been achieved and so very grateful to everyone.

The changes to all their lives had now started; the events were in their infancy, but they would now begin to affect them all.

Chapter Twenty-Two

Felicity had many thoughts running through her mind – she was concerned about James and his choice of career – but she pushed them aside. Simon had given his consent; he was the one who'd been so much against it initially, and she should surely trust his judgement.

She dragged her thoughts back to her own uncertainties. She was happy with the children, loved her husband, but she didn't have the contentment that had always been with her until recently. The twins were at school, James was at college, Myles was asleep and Simon was at work. Now was the time to sort herself out, she decided.

She stood up and ran up the stairs to her sitting room. Standing in front of the picture she'd painted of Simon, she looked at it critically. Minutes later, she sat in her rocking chair, forcing her mind back to when she had first come to Little Trenchard. *That's it*, she thought, *That's it! Now I know what I need to do!*

Galvanised into action, she went into Myles's room; he was stirring and starting to wake up, but he would be fine for a few moments longer. She ran downstairs, picked up the phone and rang Jeannie, hoping she would be in. "It's Felicity; are you around for a while? May I come over? I have something I want to discuss with you."

"Yes, fine," Jeannie said, caught up with the excitement in Felicity's voice. "The kettle will be on, or do you want something stronger?"

"I'll be over in a few minutes, and tea will be fine!"

Felicity fetched Myles from his cot, packed some food and milk for him, and then set off for Jeannie's.

By the time she got there, her excitement and enthusiasm had grown; she just hoped Jeannie would be pleased with her idea.

Once settle at Jeannie's and while she fed Myles with his bottle, Felicity began to explain, "For a few years, we've just rented out the workshop to some local clubs on the basis that it's there on the odd occasion when they needed it."

Jeannie looked somewhat puzzled. "Yes, it has worked OK, so what's different now?"

"Now, I think we should reopen it and have regular classes. What do you think?"

Astounded, Jeannie took a few moments to answer. "I'm not sure. Have we got the time? Are we able to commit to it?"

Felicity had thought all this out, so she patiently explained to Jeannie her idea. "James has his future planned and will soon be at university, the twins are at school, Myles is starting playschool shortly, Janine is at secondary school, Bella is married and Seb is off to New Zealand." She stopped to take a deep breath and watched Jeannie's expression change. "We can start art, needlework and knitting classes again. They would be on specific days at specific times, and we could finish before school ends. Also, we wouldn't have classes during school holidays."

Jeannie had caught the eagerness in Felicity's voice and was mulling over what she'd said; thoughts rushed through her mind. Felicity was right, her children were growing up, and soon, only Janine would be at home. What would she do with her time? Abe would want her to be happy, not just to while away her time with nothing constructive to do. He would encourage her in anything she wanted to do.

Smiling brightly at Felicity, Jeannie suggested, "Let's work through this idea; we can make plans and schedules, go and inspect the workshop (which we haven't done for ages), and see what needs doing and any other things which we may need attention. Oh, and we should sort all this out so we can advertise our new venture before we tell Abe and Simon." She jumped off her chair, rushed over to Felicity, hugged her and said, "This calls for a glass of wine!"

They spent the next hour discussing and jotting down the jobs to do, things they may need, details regarding advertising and the people to contact, but most importantly, they planned a trip to the workshop.

*

When Felicity arrived home with Myles, having stopped to collect the twins on the way, she then settled down to plan and jot down the ideas they'd discussed and then put them in some semblance of order. When that was done, she decided to call those clubs that occasionally rented the workshop in order to explain that, in future, they would only be able to rent it on a regular basis. She hummed as she worked, happy that she had a definite purpose back in her life.

*

Jeannie too was very upbeat as she arrived home. She was thinking about all Felicity had said. Their two eldest children would soon both have left home and Janine was growing up. They had three bedrooms in the house, plus the extension that Bella and Seb had lived in. What were they to do with all that space? A sudden thought came to mind: *Why don't we rent the annexe out?* Maybe they could think of someone they already knew. It was self-contained and private, and all they would need to do was to block the door through from the house. Yes, she liked this idea; she also had an inkling about some tenants whom they could rent it to. She would find Abe, as they had some things to discuss.

Chapter Twenty-Three

Felicity was engrossed with her plans for the reopening of the workshop and hadn't heard Simon come up to her sitting room. He stopped in the doorway and watched her as she concentrated on the work she was doing.

"Where's Myles?" Simon asked, making Felicity jump.

She dropped some papers onto the floor, and Simon bent down swiftly to pick them up. As he stood up again, he looked at the papers he was holding and frowned slightly. He held them out to Felicity.

She flushed as she took them from him. "He's with Jeannie."

"What?" said Simon.

"Myles. He's with Jeannie," repeated Felicity.

Simon sat down, looking intently at Felicity and waiting for her to speak.

"It's plans," she blurted out. "Plans for Jeannie and me to reopen the workshop for classes again.

We both need something to do." She stopped, feeling her explanation was inadequate and sounded feeble. She sighed, preparing to start her explanation again. Simon, smiling as he got up to cuddle her, "Don't worry, darling, I'm pleased you've found something you can embrace and get your teeth into. I knew there was something going on. Just remember that if there's anything I can do to help, just say so. By the way, I had a drink with Abe last night; he's also aware you and Jeannie are up to something. Perhaps you could tell Jeannie about his awareness too."

Still smiling, he went downstairs and, as he got to the front door, called out that he was going to fetch Myles.

Amazed, Felicity sat there for a few minutes after she'd heard Simon go out. On realising what he'd said, she tidied the papers and went downstairs to get tea ready. She then chuckled to herself when she recognised that both she and Jeannie had underestimated their husbands. It was also a great relief to know that they could both rely on their husbands' help.

*

Meanwhile, Jeannie had spoken to Abe about the extension on their house, and suggested that they could maybe let it to private tenants, thus relieving themselves of fees to pay a letting agent. Abe thought it was a great idea and set himself the task of researching the legalities, tenancy agreements and insurance. They were all busy sorting out projects to enhance their futures! There were still ongoing problems to resolve, none of which were insurmountable but were worrying, nevertheless.

---
*

James was excelling at school and seemingly on target for the grades he needed to study law. He worked hard and rarely left his cabin. He mostly ate with the family, but he didn't spend the evenings with them. Both Simon and Felicity worried about him becoming insular. Therefore, it was a real surprise to them that he announced one evening that he'd applied for a job at The Tavern, mostly washing up, but also occasionally waiting tables when they were busy. Michael had interviewed him, and even though James was old enough to make his own decisions, Michael had told him he should ask his parents if they had any objections. Both of them readily agreed to it, as it would be good for him to have contact with other people.

Justin and Seb had finally sorted out their visas and had booked their flights. They delayed leaving until after Christmas and planned to go on 29th December, ready to start their new life in the New Year. Justin had secured a job in Auckland with Goldman Sachs; several interviews in London had finally resulted in a job offer, which provided an exciting new venture after his long stint in IT. Seb was starting life on a sheep station that was about two hours away from Auckland. He had also enrolled in a correspondence course to complete his accountancy qualifications, as he'd already completed the first year.

Stan and Bella had settled into Ray's old flat well and were very happy there. It was easy for him to continue his work locally with Dave as his partner, and of course, Bella was still nursing at the local hospital.

It seemed that all of them were mapping out their futures quite happily; they were all moving on in the world, each in their own way and fending for themselves.

Chapter Twenty-Four

Katie and Cassie ran through the doorway as they got home from school; they were very excited as Mummy had told them on the way home that their new bedroom was ready!

Felicity quickly took Myles out of his pram and followed the girls upstairs. Simon was waiting for them in her sitting room, and she could hear him telling the twins that they had to wait for Mummy and Myles, then he would show them their new room.

However, Felicity had only reached the top stair when the girls ran across the landing and opened the door to their new bedroom. They stopped on the threshold and gazed in awe at the scene before them. Simon had worked so hard to make it very special, having made cupboards to fit around and above each bed, with a small cabinet on one side and a small table to the other for both beds. He'd offset the beds on each side of the room to make the best use of the space, and in the middle of the room, he'd fitted a double desk with drawers at each end for their crayons or whatever. Felicity had made new curtains and cushions to match in their favourite colours, which didn't clash, fortunately!

It took Simon and Felicity quite a while to persuade the girls to come down for their tea; they did eventually, but only on the promise that Myles wouldn't be allowed in their room!

It took a while after tea, but Simon finally managed to get the girls to sleep. Felicity had been settling Myles down and thinking that the next thing to do would be to move Myles into the twins' old room. It would be a wrench not to have him with her and Simon, but he was now ready to have his own room; maybe then she might get a full night's sleep.

She had just gone downstairs when Simon appeared in the kitchen. He looked tired and weary, which wasn't really surprising considering he had spent the last few days working constantly on the twins' room.

A sudden thought came to her. "We must stop saying, 'the twins,' when we want Cassie and Katie, as they do, after all, have names!"

Simon smiled at her and moved round to hug her. "On that note," he declared, "We must have another party and have the children christened. Katie, Cassie and Myles – and perhaps even Janine at the same time, if Abe and Jeannie are agreeable. It seems to me like a good excuse for a celebration!"

Felicity reached up to kiss Simon. "What a good idea," she agreed, "I'm seeing Jeannie tomorrow, so I'll suggest it to her. We are going to the workshop to check on everything and to make notes on anything we might need and also things we don't."

Simon smiled again, nodding his assent, "Don't forget to let me know if there's anything else you may need building, Abe and I can do that for you." With that, he went out to the garden.

Felicity busied herself with getting on with dinner. It was one of the nights James worked at The Tavern, so it would be just the two of them. It seemed quite strange now: James was working, Justin and Seb were flying to New Zealand soon, Bella and Stan were in Ray's old flat, and Abe and Jeannie were busy decorating the extension. *I wonder…?* thought Felicity. Jeannie had been strangely reticent about the subject; Felicity resolved to ask her tomorrow.

The kitchen door opened, and Felicity turned around to see Simon standing there with a stunned look on his face.

"What is it?" Felicity asked worriedly.

"I've just seen Abe; he called in to say that he'd a letter from Ray's solicitor. It was sent to them with a copy in it for us. It's to tell us what our inheritance is from Ray's Will. Probate has been granted."

Felicity sat down heavily, her first thought being of Ray and the finality of probate being granted. Then she looked up at Simon. "Do you know what he left us?" she asked.

Simon finally came into the kitchen. "No, I don't," he said, "however, Abe and Jeannie are coming over with the letters."

Chapter Twenty-Five

A couple of hours later, Simon, Felicity, Abe and Jeannie were trying to absorb the information they'd received from the solicitor. They were all stunned by the legacies that Ray had left them. Simon got up to find a bottle of champagne to toast Ray and to celebrate their good fortune. Felicity and Jeannie shed some tears at the loss of such a wonderful and generous man.

Ray had left his car to Simon to "do whatever he wished". It was an old, classic vintage car. Simon immediately planned to restore it completely and keep it! Abe had inherited Ray's extensive music collection, plus all his old books. They'd always been a source of interest to Abe, so he was absolutely thrilled at becoming the custodian of such a wonderful collection.

None of them had been remotely aware that Ray had kept all his late wife's jewellery. For years, it had been stored at the bank in their vault; he had never mentioned it, and now Felicity and Jeannie would inherit this. The jewellery was to be shared between them, and they could keep or sell it, whatever was their choice. As it was currently in the custody of the solicitors, they were advised to phone and make arrangements to collect it at their convenience.

Also, it transpired that Lucy and Michael had been informed of Ray's wishes and had consequently arranged for the car, books and music collection to be put into a storage unit, and they were aware that the jewellery was being held by the solicitors. Abe and Simon were advised they should contact Michael to arrange tocollect the items.

The last part of the letter was a personal message to all four of them:

I have treasured knowing you all, loved you all; you gave me great happiness and wonderful "grandchildren". For that, I give you these gifts. I know you'll care for them as I did, and I thank you all for everything.

My eternal love,

Ray

Felicity and Jeannie shed more tears, whilst Simon and Abe shared time together as they replenished the drinks.

It was both a happy and a sad time, but none of them had expected to inherit anything at all! They all felt as though they'd been blessed just by knowing Ray – that was their greatest memory.

They were still mulling over the news they'd received when James arrived home from The Tavern. He'd seen the lights were still on in the house and wanted to know whether there was a problem. He was soon told the reason why they were still up.

Abe and Jeannie then rushed off home, hoping Seb had seen Janine off to bed OK, not having realised it was so late.

Simon and Felicity sat with James for a while, having a coffee together. It had been some time since he'd spent time with his parents in such an adult way; it made him feel so comfortable and at ease with them, with the realisation that at last he could now talk about Pops without feeling guilty. He now felt; remember the good times, and there had been many of them! He could smile again!

He smiled as he said good night, and then he walked over to the cabin and, for the first time in months, went to sleep peacefully.

Chapter Twenty-Six

Felicity took Myles to playschool and then went off to meet Jeannie for their workshop inspection.

When she arrived at the house to pick up Jeannie, Abe was spending time sorting out the extension and making ready for their new tenants. Seb had moved back into his old room in the main house as he and Justin were leaving for New Zealand soon, which then gave his father free rein to complete all the necessary work, including blocking the door through to the main house.

Jeannie and Felicity set off together, and as soon as they arrived at the workshop, they spent several moments assessing the whole area and deciding how to arrange it in such a way so that each craft had its own specific space. It took a while, but eventually, they had each area planned to their satisfaction.

Felicity took the chance to ask Jeannie why she was being so mysterious about their extension, as she hadn't said anything, which wasn't like her. "Are you expecting again?" Felicity blurted out.

Jeannie spluttered then started to laugh. "Good Lord, *no!* I wanted another baby, but Abe quite rightly said that – as we have three lovely, healthy children – we're happy as we are. We're going to rent it out. We've just about got all the paperwork ready, and our prospective tenants have given notice to their current Landlord."

"You already have new tenants?" Felicity enquired. "Do we know them or are they new to the area?"

Jeannie smiled at Felicity. "It's Dave and Vanessa; they wanted a bigger place, so we offered them our extension. They're so thrilled. Abe's doing quite a lot of work to re-jig the layout, and they're hoping to move in at the end of this year, after Christmas."

"That's great! Is Dave helping Abe with the alterations?"

Jeannie grinned again and explained that he was helping Abe as and when he had time free from the projects he and Stan were currently involved with. Everything was going well for them, and they were looking forward to their new venture as Landlords.

"Come on, we must get on with our planning; there's lots to do, and we must get it all sorted if we want to be in a position to start in the New Year!"

By the end of the day, plans were in place, lists of items that would be required had been written up, advertisements were drafted and quotes from insurance companies had been requested.

Both Felicity and Jeannie were exhausted; thankfully, Abe and Simon had agreed between them to do the school runs in the afternoon, and they were also preparing dinner for everyone back at Simon's Fel.

Once everyone had arrived, they had a lively evening. The children were all excited to be together, Seb and James decamped to the cabin, and the younger ones likewise went to Kate and Cassie's room, even including Myles!

*

The next few weeks were very busy, with Abe completing the renovations to the extension, Simon doing the alterations in the workshop, and Stan and Dave assisting them both by working evenings and weekends to help complete the works. The cupboards, shelves and desks that Simon had originally made were being repurposed to fit in with the new plans. More were made to maximise the use of the areas. Jeannie arranged all the administration involved with starting their craft classes and spent time shopping for all the items they would need.

With everyone being so busy, they had almost forgotten that Christmas was nearly upon them until James came home one evening with the news that Lucy and Michael had decided to close The Tavern on Christmas Day, and that the two whole families had been invited to spend the day with them. Felicity and Simon immediately asked James to stay with the children, who were in bed, while they went to The Tavern to thank Lucy and Michael and to offer their help.

*

As they arrived there, Abe and Jeannie followed them in, having had the same idea!

Lucy and Michael ushered them through to their sitting room, distributed drinks to everyone and then proceeded to explain the idea behind their invite.

"We decided it would be a good idea to have Christmas together as Justin and Seb will be leaving us all, so we thought we could give them a good send-off," Michael suggested.

Lucy then carried on, saying, "Both your families are all invited, and we're asking Dave and Vanessa too. It should be a great day, and no one will need to bring a bottle!"

Michael then added, "The chef has the day off, so Justin and I will do the dinner, and we thought that perhaps the ladies could get together to provide the desserts."

"What a lovely idea!" Jeannie exclaimed. "We can all have a great party together to wish Justin and Seb "Bon Voyage" and to toast the lovely Pops for the good fortune and memories he has left to us all."

Everyone cheered and raised their glasses.

Sandra called through from the bar to tell them that Bella and Stan had just come in.

Michael went through to the bar and called them over: "Come and join us; we're so pleased to see you."

Smiling, they came through and sat down, joining in with the happy atmosphere after being told of the plans for Christmas Day.

Finally, when silence descended, Bella said with a very happy smile on her face, "Stan and I decided we couldn't go on saying we lived in Ray's flat, so we asked Dad to make us a plaque for our front door; which he brought with him while they were on their way here tonight, and which we've brought with us to show you all." Excitedly, she took it out. "What do you think?"

The beautifully stained wooden sign simply stated "Pops' Place".

Chapter Twenty-Seven

Everyone in the room started talking at once. Abe was congratulated for the quality of his woodwork and sign writing, Bella and Stan were thanked for thinking of the name, and everyone was hugging each other! It was the finale to a lovely day and evening.

Justin came in from the bar, immensely pleased that all his and Seb's friends and family would be together for their send-off. He had mixed feelings, but he knew it was what he wanted to do. It was also a comfort to know that he had a travel companion; even though Seb was considerably younger, they'd always been friends. Seb was like the younger brother he'd never had.

As quiet had descended on The Tavern with everyone now having gone, Justin helped his parents to clear up, and then Michael brought through a nightcap for the three of them as they sat comfortably together, not saying much as no words were necessary.

—
*
—

Simon and Felicity waved to Abe and Jeannie as they parted company, James jumped to his feet as they came through the front door. "They've all been asleep since you left and are still asleep now." He then pecked his mum on the cheek and went off to go to his cabin whistling, much happier than he had been for quite a while.

Felicity went to check on the children while Simon made them coffee, taking the mugs through to Felicity's sitting room, sat down with a contented sigh. A few months ago, life had been in a mess for most of them, but as time had gone by they'd all realised they could pursue other interests and still be content and happy.

As Felicity came into the room, he turned and smiled at her. "Come here and sit with me, darling; there's something I would like to tell you."

Felicity smiled in response and curled up on his lap. She looked longingly at him and waited for him to speak.

"I just wanted to tell you how much I love you, always," he stated.

He picked her up and laid her on the carpet, just as he had all those years ago, the first time he'd made love to her. Surprised but with passion equal to his, she too was remembering that time and how she'd felt. It had been a long time since they'd made love in such a passionate and intense way. Words were not necessary as Simon's beautiful, sparkling, silvery eyes told her everything she needed to know.

Chapter Twenty-Eight

Simon woke up to hear Felicity calling out in distress; she was tossing and turning in the bed, and the bedclothes were awry.

"Simon! Simon! I forgot! I should have remembered. I must go and sort it out now." She tried to disentangle herself from the rumpled bed.

Simon quickly turned on the light and went round the bed to hold her tightly, trying to calm her down.

After a few moments, she relaxed and went quiet as she realised Simon was hugging her to him. "What is it? What's happened? Have I been dreaming?" As she was talking she became quieter and removed herself from Simon's arm as her memory returned to her. "I was dreaming. I'd forgotten all about having the children christened; I was supposed to talk to Jeannie about it. I completely forgot!" She laughed shakily and smiled weakly at Simon.

"What a silly thing to get upset about! We can do it at any time, can't we?" Simon was so relieved.

He smiled reassuringly at her, straightened the bed clothes and went to make a hot drink for them both. He had no idea why Felicity had been so upset, but she seemed OK now, and he resolved he wouldn't mention it to her unless she brought the subject to his attention. When he got back upstairs, she was asleep, quiet and peaceful. He took his cocoa into Felicity's sitting room, knowing he wouldn't settle for a while.

He sat there, thinking about the events of the last half hour. He had no explanation, none whatsoever, so he decided to keep it to himself. The children hadn't woken up, so they knew nothing. It would all be best left alone. He went back to bed, Felicity was still fast asleep, climbed in carefully and, to his surprise, was asleep almost immediately.

---
*

Felicity stretched her stiff limbs; she must have been restless last night. She turned to reach for Simon, but he wasn't there; he must already be up. She looked at the clock. "Good grief, it's almost 8am!"

She shot out of bed and went to get the girls up, but their beds were empty and made, with their clothes gone; Myles wasn't in his room either. She then heard laughter from the kitchen.

She went downstairs, and as she entered the kitchen, she saw Myles in his highchair, trying to spoon cereal into his mouth, which was the reason for the laughter. He missed his mouth every time, which the twins found really funny. Consequently, there was more cereal on the highchair than in his bowl. Simon was chuckling too; he motioned to Felicity to sit down and then brought her a cup of coffee. He kissed the top of her head and his silver-specked eyes caused a blush to spread across her cheeks.

Cassie immediately squealed out, "Why have you gone all red, Mummy?"

"It's the hot coffee, that's all," Felicity croaked. She darted a look at Simon, who had raised his eyebrows and his eyes had darkened. She jumped up and said to no one in particular, "I have to do the school run."

"Stay there, darling; I'll do that this morning," Simon offered. "I have to go to the workshop to finish the new shelves. You looked so peaceful this morning that I didn't want to wake you. I'll take Myles to playschool too."

Felicity sat down at the table again, thinking about what to do with the unexpected free time. She would ring Jeannie; they must get the christening sorted out. *Now what made me think of that?* She thought suddenly. Shaking her head, she turned when Simon came back into the room, by which time the children were all ready to go. She kissed them all and ushered them all outside.

At the last moment, Simon turned round, grabbed Felicity and kissed her passionately. She gasped as he let her go, her legs shaking.

He mouthed at her, "I love you," and then followed the children down the path.

Shakily, Felicity went back to the table and marvelled at the fact Simon could still affect her that way. *Get hold of yourself,* she told herself, *There are things to do.* First of all, she was to call Jeannie, make plans to meet her and then see Lucy about the Christmas arrangements.

$\overline{\underset{=}{*}}$

An hour later, Jeannie was listening to Felicity's ideas about the christening of their children. They were both happy to have a joint celebration and agreed on a buffet lunch, which Jeannie would host. First, though, the date must be settled; however, they both agreed to wait until the New Year, as Justin and Seb's send-off was the priority at the moment.

Jeannie decided to walk to The Tavern with Felicity; they could then discuss Christmas and be sure that Lucy had enough help. Once there, they had a lovely lunchtime and sorted everything out between them. It was a successful day. Abe had completed all the renovations in the extension, so they had a celebratory drink. They were all so excited that, at last, they had things to celebrate.

$\overline{\underset{=}{*}}$

Felicity went back to Simon's Fel feeling positive, very happy, serene and content. It had been a while since she'd felt that good. She was singing softly to herself as she opened the door and was surprised to hear Simon's voice. She went on through to the kitchen.

Simon hadn't heard her come in, and she knew immediately that something was wrong. Simon was visibly upset. He put the phone down and put his head in his hands, his whole body trembling. She rushed towards him, thinking he was going to collapse.

As Felicity reached him, he fell into her embrace, hugging her tightly. For a while she stood with him.

He then led her to a chair and settled her onto his lap. "Please don't say anything until I've finished, then ask me any questions you like." He took a deep breath and continued, "I have no family any more, but I've just had a call from London. Apparently, the solicitor who dealt with all my father's affairs has been trying to find me because I'm the sole beneficiary – there's no one else. I'm stunned and a bit sceptical. I have to look into all this, but not now – not at this time. Probably after Christmas when things are quieter. Now, I'm even less sure about James's career choice, so I'll chat to him again, but later." He sighed heavily and studied Felicity's expression.

She was silent for a few moments, then said, "I have so many questions, Simon, but they can wait. I agree that now is not the time; after Christmas would be better. Please just take care when you speak to James, he's so set on being a lawyer."

Events were going to take a strange turn; no one could have foreseen the outcome.

Chapter Twenty-Nine

Melissa dropped her bags on the floor, picked up the post from the doormat and went straight through to the kitchen. Nothing had changed; everything was as normal – neat and tidy, with nothing out of place. What exactly had she expected? It was just like her mother to make sure it was all pristine, even though she had been going into hospital. Irritated by the situation she found herself in, she opened the cupboard where her mother kept the wine and poured herself a large glass.

She sat at the spotless table and let her eyes wander around the room. How could her mother have died just like that? It was so inconvenient; there would be so much to do, and she was too busy! She sighed again, not thinking that she was in any way being selfish or unfeeling.

Suddenly remembering the pile of post she'd picked up, she went to retrieve it from the worktop where she'd dropped it after coming into the flat. After sitting down again and sipping her wine, she leafed idly through it, her eyebrows rising in surprise when she saw the envelope that was emblazoned with the name of a London firm of solicitors across the top.

She opened it quickly, and inside was a letter requesting that she contact them as soon as possible for the reading of her mother's Will. Startled, she studied it for some time until, abruptly galvanised into action, she found her mobile to ring their office. About to dial the number, she realised that she ought to gather her thoughts, as she should sound a bit more respectful and upset than she actually felt – rather than being excited about what she might inherit!

She soon found it was two days before they had an available appointment, but that would give her time to plan her story, as she hadn't gone immediately to the hospital when her mother died. Melissa had delayed her departure from Bristol University; she wanted to complete the term to make sure her attendance record was 100%. Her mother was dead, and she wasn't the weeping-and-wailing type. The hospital had stated they would keep her mother in the mortuary until Melissa advised them that undertakers would be collecting the body. Therefore, it was about a week later that Melissa had finally called the hospital to say she was home from University and would be making the necessary arrangements during the next few days.

After having spent time with the funeral director to arrange a cremation, Melissa turned her attention to planning her trip to London. She booked a room in a small hotel near the solicitors office.

---
*

On the appointed day, Melissa travelled to London, and once booked into the hotel, she went to keep her appointment with the solicitor, suitably dressed in smart, sombre clothes. One thing her mother had taught her was to always dress appropriately.

Sitting opposite, the solicitor, Mr Graham Tatchell (his name was carved smartly on a wooden plaque on his desk), she tried to keep a demure and solemn expression on her face. However, excitement was bubbling inside her.

"To summarise, Miss Cartwright, you are the sole beneficiary. The property in Bristol has no mortgage on it and is leasehold, although your mother did own the freehold of the building, which will also come to you. All your mother's chattels and belongings are yours, as are the contents of the flat. In fact, everything your mother owned is now yours to do with as you wish. Your education expenses will continue to be paid until you attain the age of twenty-five. There's a trust fund for this set up and arranged by your father, and any funds remaining after your twenty-fifth birthday will then pass to you. I believe there will be a small monetary inheritance from that Trust." Mr Tatchell stopped speaking and was obviously waiting for Melissa's response.

"Thank you so much for explaining it all to me. I'll be in touch if I have any queries. One question: do you know the name of the person who set up the Trust Fund for my education?"

"Yes, I do. It's all explained in the Will, a copy of which I shall give you today, but please don't hesitate to call me should you require any further explanation or assistance in dealing with your mother's estate." Mr Tatchell then stood up, came round his desk and handed Melissa a large folder of papers." Goodbye, Miss Cartwright; it was a pleasure to meet you."

Melissa shook his hand and left his office. With the papers tucked carefully into her large bag, she swiftly made her way back to the hotel. As soon as she was in her room, she quickly opened the folder, took out the papers inside and leafed through them until she found the document she was hoping to find.

This was the document showing a Trust Fund had been recorded to pay for the education of Melissa Cartwright until she attains the age of twenty-five years, to be paid for by Mr Geoffrey James QC.

Chapter Thirty

A malicious smile spread gleefully across Melissa's face. She was now aware who her father was, so she could now make plans! She must go through all her mother's papers very carefully, write down all the relevant information, collate it all and start her search.

First, though, she would return to the flat in Bristol and concentrate on making it her own – in her own style. She had the money, thanks to her mother, even though she considered it was hers anyway by right!

Nothing could stop her now! She was determined to finish her law studies, then further her education, study for a degree, set her sights on becoming a barrister attain the, which would need further study to pass the bar exam, maybe even become a QC! The thought that she could same heights in her chosen profession as her unknown father excited her. She made a mental note to contact the firm of lawyers he'd owned, investigate the working of the firm and find out everything about him – even the dark side. He must have had one; after all, he had impregnated her mother, and she was the living proof of that.

Melissa ordered a meal from room service and spent the rest of the evening packing for her journey back to Bristol and planning how she would alter the flat to suit her own needs.

*

Christmas frustrated Melissa's plans: she couldn't arrange for any work to be done as everywhere was closed for the holiday. However, she had organised her mother's funeral, which would be a very quiet affair as there was no one but Melissa herself to attend the service. She arranged for the ashes to be scattered, as she wasn't remotely religious and didn't want any memorial to visit. As soon as it was all over, she walked away, her mother already forgotten.

Fortunately, she was due back at Bristol University in three weeks. She spent her time shopping for new furniture, bedding and towels. All the old furniture was collected by a house clearance company, and her mother's clothes were sent to Oxfam. The only thing Melissa kept was the paperwork she found. Having emptied the flat and with nowhere to stay, she rented a fully furnished property on a short lease. This gave her the time and freedom and keep anything that could be of possible use to her.

By the time Melissa needed to return to University, she'd formulated a plan to take her revenge on the man whom she now thought of as the one who had defiled her mother and been forced into paying his due to the child he'd fathered.

The information she had about this man and his family was safely locked away; she would take her time, plot her revenge and act at the appropriate moment.

Satisfied with all she had learnt, she left her temporary home, dropped off the key with the agent and started on her journey back to University. She would return at Easter, by which time the flat should be completed, reformed, refurnished and redecorated. She was very much looking forward to instigating her revengeful plans.

She would spend her time unravelling Geoffrey James's family tree. She had noted down the places she needed to visit. They had some cute names, two of which came immediately to mind: Little Trenchard and Middle Trenchard. She would enjoy visiting them.

Chapter Thirty-One

The time had gone by so quickly; they were all exhausted, but their hard work was now complete. Justin and Seb had packed in readiness for emigrating to New Zealand. James was excelling at Sixth Form College and thoroughly enjoying his job at The Tavern. Dave and Vanessa were staying with Stan and Bella for a few days until they moved into the extension at Abe and Jeannie's house.

Everyone was looking forward to the party on Christmas Day. Bella and Vanessa had joined forces to decorate the dining room at The Tavern in readiness for the day.

Abe, Jeannie, Simon and Felicity were all together at Simon's Fel, feeling tired but happy. Justin, Seb and James were in The Tavern; Seb was staying there until they flew to New Zealand on 30th December. All their plans had worked out for them without too many hiccups.

Felicity and Jeannie had a few things to finish in the

workshop before they started their new classes. They were all sitting together discussing what they should call themselves, as The Workshop sounded as being too utilitarian – this having been Abe's comment. Felicity and Jeannie had burst out laughing at his use of words, but Simon had interjected to say he agreed with Abe and they needed something a bit grander! They all looked at each other, waiting for a sensible suggestion to be put forward.

In the silence, Janine appeared asking for a drink and enquiring why they were all looking so serious. While Jeannie went to fetch her a drink, Janine furrowed her brow and joined the others in thought. Muttered suggestions were being tossed about and then immediately dismissed.

Janine suddenly stood up, smiling happily, as she took the drink her mother had just offered her. "How about "The Hobby Loft?" she suggested over her shoulder as she walked out of the room, heading back to Cassie and Katie's bedroom, as she was staying for a sleepover with the twins.

Stunned, they all looked at the lounge door through which Janine had just disappeared, then they all started to talk at once:

"How did she think of that?"

"Where did that come from?"

"What a great idea!"

"Could you make us a special sign, Abe?" This last comment came from Jeannie as she looked questioningly at her husband.

"Of course," he said, "I'd be delighted."

Jeannie rushed upstairs to tell Janine that they'd adopted her suggestion.

Almost asleep, she smiled at Jeannie saying, "I'm glad you all liked it". Jeannie hugged her daughter and then left the three girls sleeping happily.

Back down in the lounge, she found Simon had opened some champagne and was handing out a glass to each of them. They all raised their glasses.

Abe said, "To all of us in our new ventures and to Ray, our best friend."

It was a happy moment to end the evening on. They had a lovely party to go to tomorrow, knowing it was going to be a terrific send-off for Justin and Seb.

Felicity and Simon, Abe and Jeannie all hugged each other and then went off to bed, glad that they were sharing this evening and tomorrow together.

Abe and Jeannie settled down on the sofa bed in Felicity's sitting room; Abe held Jeannie in his arms, and whispered to her: "I know Seb is leaving us in a few days' time, but I promise you we'll visit him and take Janine with us."

"Thank you, darling; Janine will love that."

Over the past year, so much had changed for them and their families. Jeannie settled contentedly in Abe's arms. *Everything is going so well,* she thought, *there can only be good times ahead.*

Chapter Thirty-Two

Christmas Day started early for them. The girls woke up to find stockings had been left for them by "Father Christmas". Excitedly, they opened the presents and then rushed downstairs to show their parents; James joined them having opened his own presents in the cabin.

Breakfast was noisy but great fun. It took a while to calm the children, but eventually, they all set off, laden with more presents for everyone at The Tavern. Katie and Cassie skipped alongside Janine, each holding a new teddy bear and trying to decide what to call them. The adults followed behind, each lost in their own thoughts.

James was walking beside Felicity and suddenly said, "Mum, thanks so much for the camera equipment and book token – just what I needed. Thanks too for your understanding. I had a bad time after Pops died, but I'm OK now and looking forward to my law studies."

He took off at a run after the girls, as they were starting to argue about names for the teddies. He gathered them together and explained they were on their way to a party. "Cheer up, girls, we'll sort out names later; we're off to have some fun."

The girls giggled and went off with James as he zigzagged along the road, telling them the fun started now!

Felicity had been startled by James's words; he didn't often talk so candidly. Once again, he'd surprised her with his desire to be a lawyer, but she wouldn't think about it today. Tomorrow, she would speak to Simon. She glanced at him now; he was relaxed and happy, smiling at Abe and Jeannie's tales of Seb as a baby. Today was for Seb and Justin – everything else could wait.

*

Hours later, everyone was full of a wonderful Christmas lunch. The youngsters were all having a nap upstairs, and the talk turned to Justin and Seb's imminent move to New Zealand, which was now only a few days away. Both Lucy and Jeannie were upset that they were emigrating, but the women fully understood that their sons had to make their own decisions in life. They agreed to travel next year during the school holidays in Summer and spend a few weeks with Justin and Seb. Janine would go too; it would be a real adventure for her and educational too!

James volunteered to move into The Tavern for the duration of the visit; he would be home from College then and could house sit. Simon would help James with the heavy work at The Tavern, and Lucy had already asked Sandra if she would be prepared to work every day to run the bar alongside James.

Michael decided they wouldn't employ a replacement chef while they were away; instead, it was arranged that Sandra and James would manage between them with a simple "Sandwich Menu", as he felt that, after all, anyone could make a decent sandwich! Michael would display a notice to inform everyone that hot food wouldn't be available during their absence in New Zealand.

With everyone in agreement, the party continued until late; the children – having been put upstairs – slept through it all. It was the early hours of Boxing Day when Simon and Felicity as well as Abe and Jeannie made their respective ways to their homes. James stayed at The Tavern, promising to bring the children who were still asleep, home in the morning. Young Myles slept in Simon's arms as they walked home, all content and happy, knowing there would be adventure for them all in the New Year.

On 29thDecember, they were all at The Tavern seeing Seb and Justin off to New Zealand. The two young men were feeling sad but happy at the prospect before them; however, knowing that their families were planning to come and visit them in the Summer was a real boost.

The Tavern was in full swing again, with everyone looking forward to the New Year's Eve celebrations the next day. James was thoroughly enjoying his "promotion" to bartender and looking forward to starting College. His grades had been excellent, so his place at Bristol University had been confirmed. He didn't want to take a gap year; he was too keen to begin his studies.

Dave and Vanessa were moving into the extension at Abe and Jeannie's house on 1st January (their choice!) as they had a couple of weeks' holiday to settle in.

Excitement was abundant in the village; it was New Year's Eve, and everyone was happy and smiling with most of the villagers gathered at The Tavern for the celebrations.

Two very joyful couples spread their own happy news with their friends. Michael rang the pub bell to announce to everyone that Bella and Stan, along with Dave and Vanessa, were all expectant parents! Their babies were due around the same time, about six months ahead. It was a very happy time for everyone, and the party turned into a very joyful celebratory gathering.

Chapter Thirty-Three

Life quietly moved on in Little Trenchard, although very busy for everyone. All the students in Felicity and Jeannie's classes at The Hobby Loft were involved in making baby clothes, toys and furniture for the new arrivals. Abe stepped smoothly into the role of advisor for furniture-making. Simon was busy decorating and altering spaces to be nurseries for the new babies. Stan and Dave worked all hours at their business, building up nest eggs to help when their respective wives had to stop working.

James went off to London to complete his work experience at the Law firm, although he spent most of his time filing and tea-making, but he found it enthralling. He listened intently to the conversations he heard between clients and solicitors, and even went to Court several times, taking notice of everything that happened and making notes of the way lawyers conducted their briefs. He found it fascinating and became more and more determined to succeed in his chosen career.

Back home, unbeknown to him, his mother and father were vehemently discussing that very subject. Simon was still unsure about James making that decision. He was unsettled; he couldn't understand why it disturbed him so much. Felicity had more faith in James's choice, even though her own experience at the hands of Gordon James had been despicable. She tried hard to win Simon round, but he wouldn't listen to her; he had a deep-seated worry that the James family would cause problems for them. The death of his father had renewed his doubt about the security of their home. Ray had assured him that the ownership of Simon's Fel was watertight, but he still worried. He forced a smile to his face and told Felicity he was probably worrying unduly. She smiled back, kissed him and went out of the room. He heard her singing softly, happy in her work. He resolved to have the deeds and title for their property checked thoroughly, just to put his mind at rest and to ensure it was secure for his family.

James, meanwhile, having finished his work placement, threw himself into studying hard at home, preparing for starting at University. This was interspersed with the thoughts of the people he had met in London – especially Melissa; he had liked her!

It seemed only a short while later, but suddenly the Summer holidays were upon them. James moved into The Tavern, Michael had taught Simon the intricacies of changing barrels and cleaning pipes, Felicity was spending the Summer refreshing The Hobby Loft, and in between all of this, they were anxiously awaiting the births of Bella's and Vanessa's babies.

Felicity was busy baking when Jeannie burst through the door.

"Bella has gone into labour, Abe's driving her to the hospital, and Stan is picking me up on his way," Jeannie explained. "Will you keep Janine here, please? I've called the school, and they'll make sure she knows to come here." Jeannie then turned and ran out to wait for Stan.

Felicity called, "Good luck," after her, just as Stan arrived.

Jeannie got into the car, and then as they sped off she waved to Felicity with a look of excitement and worry on her face.

A few moments later, Simon came in with a questioning look at Felicity. "I've just seen Jeannie with Stan; she was waving madly. Has something happened?"

Felicity relayed the last few moments, telling Simon that she hadn't actually spoken to Jeannie; she'd just listened and then she ran off! Simon smiled, gave her a quick kiss and went out, remembering his own reaction to fatherhood.

Janine arrived back from school, but realised before Felicity informed her why she'd been sent there. "I'm going to be Aunty Janine," she said, "What a mouthful for a baby! Maybe I'll ask Bella if I can be known as Janey; it's much easier to say. Are the girls in their room, Felicity?" She went straight out of the room and up the stairs before Felicity could answer.

Felicity just looked at the kitchen door as she went. Well! she thought, How she's grown up in a few moments. Suddenly she's decided on a new name for herself in her new role as an aunt and also decided that she can call me just Felicity! Not that I mind – she thought, they just grow up so fast. She went back to her baking, listening out for the telephone.

*

Hours later, Felicity had just put the girls to bed, Myles was asleep in his bed. Meanwhile, Simon had gone to The Tavern to assist Michael and to see how the bar worked with Sandra and James, when she received a phone call. After ending the call, she phoned Simon from home to say "Bella and Stan have a son named Matthew Ray Connors, and all is well."

When Simon told Michael, he decided the customers should enjoy a toast to the new baby on the house, staff included.

When Simon and James arrived home, Jeannie and Abe were there too. Abe had already opened the champagne, and they all toasted the baby– even Janine was allowed a small glass.

Jeannie declared, "I'm so glad the baby arrived before we go to New Zealand, though I'm worried that I won't be on hand to help Bella."

Felicity said, "I'll be here to help, she can always call on me",

They hugged each other; they'd become such good friends over the years and were always there for each other. Sometimes words weren't necessary.

Shortly afterwards, Jeannie, Abe and Janine left for home.

Jeannie raised her eyebrows as Janine said, "Goodbye, Felicity," and she waved as she walked down the path.

Felicity smiled at Jeannie and shrugged her shoulders, the understanding complete between them.

*

Two days before they left for New Zealand, Vanessa went into labour unexpectedly, and almost before Jeannie could rush into the extension, the baby was arriving! Fortunately, Abe was home too, and he called an ambulance as well as letting Dave know immediately what was happening.

By the time the ambulance arrived, Vanessa had given birth to a girl, so very quickly but without any problems. Dave arrived a few moments later, still in his overalls and work boots. He was so excited and thrilled that he burst into tears and hugged everyone there, including the paramedics. Quickly, he changed out of his work clothes and went off to the hospital with Vanessa and their daughter.

Jeannie sat down, feeling faint suddenly with the realisation dawning on her that she'd just delivered the baby! Abe brought her some brandy to steady and revive her.

"Thank God we were still here, Abe; at least now we can go to New Zealand with no worries about the babies!"

The following morning Dave and Vanessa arrived back home with their daughter, all smiles and beaming with happiness, they were greeted by Abe and Jeannie, who had tidied the living room ready for their homecoming. Abe and Jeannie soon left as they were due to depart for New Zealand the following day – and now they had good news to tell Seb and Justin.

*

Simon and Felicity waved them all off on their long journey, with some trepidation at the task they had before them. They had two new babies to watch over and a pub to keep an eye on, their son was to be the stand-in landlord. Simon had yet to decide just what he should do about the inheritance from his late father.

Chapter Thirty-Four

Simon realised he'd been very reluctant to embrace the necessity of resolving the inheritance issues caused by the death of his father. He had left it too long. The latest letter he'd received from the solicitors had politely suggested it was time the matter was settled. Sighing deeply, he went to find Felicity.

She turned round as she heard him come into her sitting room, smiling at him. The smile froze on her face, as he looked so serious, but before she could say anything, he blurted out, "I have to go to London now; I may be away for a few days, but I must go. Dave or Stan will assist if any problems arise at The Tavern. I have to sort out my father's Will; it has been left too long. It's my fault – I should have sorted it out before now. I'll call when I get there." Having said this, he turned round and went out.

She heard him in their room, gathering together the things he needed for his trip. Knowing him so well, she waited until he came back to her.

He was carrying a small suitcase and a folder of papers. He kissed her passionately, then mouthed at her, "I love you," and left.

Felicity watched him go and then ran to the window as she heard his car driving away. She stood there for a while, feeling bereft and lonely, but realising that it was necessary for him to finally settle this matter. At last, Simon had come to his senses! She turned from the window and went slowly downstairs. She would let James know where his father had gone and why, she would then explain to the children that Daddy had some urgent business in London. How she wished Jeannie was here, as she needed someone to talk to! But who? *Bella*, she thought suddenly. They'd always been close, Bella would be like her Mum, and just listen quietly. She jumped up and quickly phoned Bella, who responded that she could be with Felicity shortly, bringing the baby with her.

After checking that the children were OK in the garden, Felicity switched on the kettle and waited for Bella to arrive. Her thoughts were with Simon, wondering what the solicitor would have to say.

Bella soon arrived, she and Felicity ejoyed the afternoon together with Bella feeling very privileged that she had become the confidante that Felicity needed.

---
*

Later that evening, Felicity answered the phone, relieved to hear Simon's voice.

"I've arrived OK and have booked into a Premier Inn for two nights. I've also arranged an appointment with the solicitor for 9am tomorrow. He said it would take some time, so he's booked the whole morning with me. How are you? How are the children? I miss you so much."

"We're all fine; don't worry," she reassured him.

"Take care, darling; I'll ring you tomorrow after the meeting." The line went dead.

Felicity looked at the phone for a few moments before she realised he'd gone. Quickly, she dialled 1471 and noted down the number he had called from, and she then rushed from the room to check if he had his mobile with him. She would call him later. She knew he was worrying about the meeting, as he had sounded so upset. In the meantime, she would text him to ensure he knew she was thinking of him. When she called him later, she would tell him she loved him.

In the meantime, she called James to tell him where his Dad had gone. He told his Mum that he was glad his Dad had gone to sort out the inheritance and that all was well at The Tavern.

As she'd planned, she called Simon in the evening when the children were in bed. They then spent some while talking to each other, nothing much was said between them of the meeting the next day but both of them went to bed feeling comforted and loved.

Simon rang Felicity early the next afternoon. Firstly, this was to let her know he was returning home that night and would be there about 8pm. Secondly, he said he would explain it all when he got home, but the most important thing was that, at last, he was free of the James family and he was so glad he'd changed his name to Grantley all those years ago. He ended the call saying he would see them soon.

Relieved, Felicity told the children that Daddy would be home later, then she called James to let him know too and, finally, she rang Bella to tell her that all was well. She bustled about making dinner for the children and pasta sauce for her and Simon for when he got home. It would probably be a late night, so she put a bottle of wine in the fridge.

*

It was nearly 8.30pm when Simon arrived home. He hugged Felicity tightly, telling her how much he'd missed her. He greeted the excited children, who had been allowed to stay up to see their father.

Half an hour later, Simon and Felicity had settled the children in bed and were now both each holding a large glass of wine.

Simon explained what had happened at the meeting: "The solicitor was very informative; he explained fully the options open to me. Firstly, I was very pleased to hear that the law firm would be left in its entirety to the partners, with the assets to be shared between them. It was a fait accompli; I had no say in the matter. I was thrilled to say the least! It was to be left to the solicitor to deal with.

"There was no actual money to be left to me. His late wife would keep the property, and once she died, the monies from the sale of that property were to be left to a charity of my father's choosing. Once again, the administration of that was left to the solicitor. If I objected to any of my father's wishes, I would have to contest it. I said immediately I did not wish to do so – ever!"

Simon stopped at this point to take a drink. Felicity kept quiet and waited for Simon to go on.

"There was one item that was somewhat mysterious," he went on to explain, "If anyone made any claim within five years of the date of his death, the solicitor was to investigate the validity of the claim through the Courts and their judgement would be final."

"Simon, does that mean we're at risk with our house?" Felicity spoke urgently and worriedly, a frown spreading across her face.

"No, darling; no. I asked him that, and he said it was quite a usual sort of stipulation to be included in a Will, especially when a very successful business was involved. Besides, Ray assured us that our ownership was completely legal."

He sat back, relaxed and happy, appearing more settled than she'd seen him for a long while. She smiled too, happy that all his worries had been put to rest. She went across to him and snuggled into his lap, all thoughts of a cosy pasta supper forgotten.

Chapter Thirty-Five

James had thoroughly enjoyed his time at The Tavern, and it had mostly all gone smoothly! There had been a few dramas, but with the help of his Dad and Sandra, everything had been sorted out.

The babies were both thriving. Felicity had enjoyed her time helping Bella and Vanessa when needed. Everyone was excited at the imminent homecoming of the two families that day!

Later that day James handed the keys of The Tavern back to Michael and Lucy now that they had arrived safely home. He then went back to his cabin to prepare for starting University, he had just a week to get everything sorted out. He would join all the family at The Tavern later, when there was going to be a small party to thank the "staff" for their help. All the news was to be imparted about the visit to New Zealand.

Simon went to see James as soon as he could after he got back to the cabin. He wanted to impress on James that he fully supported his choice of career. His fears had been allayed after his trip to London, he trusted James's judgement and hoped his son would achieve everything he wanted from his chosen path in life. James was stunned, it was such a relief to him to have his father's full backing. He spontaneously hugged his Dad, thrilled to know he had the support of both his parents. Simon smiled as he went back to the cottage – at last, he had made peace with James!

*

It was a very lively party. Everyone there wanted to know how Seb and Justin were, what New Zealand was like, how were the travels, and marvelling how the babies had grown in the relatively short time they'd been away.

After much laughter and talking, it transpired that Seb had himself taken over the lease on an apartment, which he now shared with a young man he'd met in the bar he worked at. They'd immediately become friends and soon got used to living together, splitting all the costs and chores between them. It suited them both, and Seb had shelved his plans to pursue sheep farming until he'd qualified for his accountancy degree. He'd realised it would give him a better and more secure future. His friend Bryan was also studying to gain his accountancy degree, and both worked at the bar to supplement their income.

Justin had found himself a great apartment in central Auckland. He loved the hustle and bustle of the city and revelled in his new job. He had quickly shown his enthusiasm for the job and had risen in the ranks already after just a few months. His employers soon realised that his IT knowledge was formidable and increased his salary considerably.

He'd never been that interested in forming a steady relationship with a woman, but he'd met Carla, who soon became enamoured with Lucy and Michael – to the extent that Justin and Carla planned to visit his parents in Cornwall early the following spring. Justin's final words to them was to inform them that they were considering getting married in Little Trenchard. Carla insisted Lucy and Michael should meet her parents as she was an only child and had no other family. They all had a great day together, and Lucy and Michael promised to keep in touch with Carla's parents.

Things seemed to be moving along so quickly, and Janine had suggested she might think about emigrating when she had completed college and university. Abe and Jeannie listened to what she was saying, but they knew that she was living in the euphoria of the moment. She had changed her mind so often about the career she would like! It remained to be seen as to what she would finally decide to do.

Simon took James to the University; he'd decided he would live there during the week and come home for weekends. Michael had said there would always be work for him at The Tavern if he wanted it. He was looking forward to the lectures and studies, but wasn't interested in partying and living the high life that appeared to be part of Uni life. He told his Dad as they parted company that he was going to learn to drive, he would buy a small car using some of the money Ray had left him. Simon was pleasantly surprised that his son had thought so carefully about his legacy from Ray and was going to be putting part of it to such good use. He left James, sure in his mind that his son would be OK, happy in his choice of career and happy at the plans he had for his future.

When he arrived home, he was smiling, contented and enthusiastic at the future for the whole family. The twins and Myles were jumping up and down with glee as their father gathered them up to play in the garden. Felicity was astonished, as he would quite often leave it to Felicity to entertain the children.

She took a glass of wine outside and watched as they all ran around, getting muddier by the minute – including Simon.

Once back indoors, there was much laughter and fun as Simon took them off to bath and shower.

It was later on after they'd all eaten and the children had gone to bed exhausted, that Simon explained to Felicity how it would be when James got to University. "James is growing up, darling; he's going to buy a car, have driving lessons so he can drive himself to and from Uni, and he's using some of his legacy from Ray to do so. I know he's doing the right thing as he is determined to succeed. I am sure he will. He said he doesn't want to be part of the 'University high life' as he put it; he wants to study and work hard for his future."

Simon turned to Felicity and held her close in his arms. His eyes darkened and the silvery glints shone out at her. She could she the unspoken question in them, her kiss in response telling him all he needed to know.

Chapter Thirty-Six

As life continued happily in Little Trenchard, James arrived home unexpectedly one day. Felicity watched as a strange car drew up on the drive, and she let out a squeal of surprise when James climbed out of the driving seat. She ran out of the house and hugged James. "What are you doing here? Whose car is this? I didn't know you could drive. You hadn't told us you were learning!"

James disentangled himself from his mother's embrace and said laughingly, "I wanted to surprise you. I told you last weekend I was coming home for the Easter holidays! It's now Easter, so here I am! "He turned to the car and took out his suitcase and various boxes of books and papers. "I'll be busy, Mum; I have studying to do. I also have to see Michael tonight to find out when I can work for him. I have four weeks before I need to be back. How are the little ones?"

Felicity was so pleased to see James, helping him to carry his luggage and boxes to the cabin, listening earnestly to his tales of life at Uni.

Later, he went with her to collect the children from school. They were surprised and thrilled to see their big brother, and happy too that he would be home for a few weeks.

When he returned home from work, Simon was astounded to hear that James had driven himself home having passed his driving test at the first attempt. They all had a lively dinner, and as James got up from the table to go and see Michael, he asked his father to go with him so they could have a drink together. Surprised and pleased, Simon got up too, realising how much their son had grown up.

---
*

It was late when they got home; James went straight to his cabin, and Simon found Felicity dozing in her sitting room. She woke up as Simon walked in. He was smiling happily and proceeded to relay to her James's stories of his time at Uni. He had decided to take an intensive driving course, passed that and found a small runabout car to get him around. His studies were going very well, and he was trying to find out if he could shorten the process by taking extra exams early, although that would mean extra study and lectures too.

"He seems so determined, Felicity; I have to admire his work ethics. Nothing is going to get in his way! He really has matured and wants to do all he can to achieve his goal. He also told me that he takes time out from studying to keep up with his hobbies of photography and sketching. He's putting together a portfolio of his work and has ideas of getting them published! What on earth he would title it, I don't know, but he's sure he'll be successful at that too!

"Oh yes, he also mentioned a young lady he'd met – apparently in London, I think. She's a couple of years older than him also studying law, but obviously, well ahead of him in her degree. He sees her around the University, but he doesn't really know her that well. However, she must have made an impression on him as he wouldn't have mentioned her otherwise." Simon stopped talking and smiled at Felicity, remembering the impact he had felt when he first met her.

They sat companionably together, talking quietly, pleased to have their son home for a while. Felicity was mostly thinking about the mystery girl James had mentioned.

Chapter Thirty-Seven

James was working behind the bar at The Tavern when a young woman came in, came up to him, and enquired about bed and breakfast.

Stunned, James looked at her, then smiled and said, "Hello, Melissa, I never expected to see you in this neck of the woods!"

She put her bag down, smiled back slightly and asked, "Do I know you? Oh yes, I remember now – you're at Bristol Uni. I've seen you a few times, haven't I? You're in your first year, aren't you?" She paused. "I'm just taking a short break from studying and decided to come to Cornwall; I haven't been here before."

James went to fetch the diary to check if they had a spare room. He'd recovered from his initial shock of seeing her and then took her details to book her in, gave her a room key, welcomed her to The Tavern and then went to let Lucy know they had another visitor for bed and breakfast.

The bar was now getting busy, and James was kept on his toes serving the customers and helping Lucy in the dining room. He was too busy to wonder too much about Melissa, but later in the evening, she came into the bar and ordered a glass of wine. Smilingly, he served her and asked if she wanted to add it to her room bill.

"Of course," she said, "I don't carry cash!" She took her drink, then went to sit at a small table in the bar, taking a book from her bag and becoming engrossed in it.

Taken somewhat aback by the abruptness of her comment, he watched her until another customer approached. Soon, he was busy again. When he looked round for her; she had gone – presumably, to her room. He shrugged his shoulders and thought she must just have been tired from driving; he would surely see her again.

What James hadn't noticed was that Melissa had been watching him closely, turning the pages of her book occasionally to give the pretence of reading it. A few times, she'd looked at other customers when they'd stopped at her table, but the expression on her face discouraged them immediately! She waited until James was really busy and then went out of the main door. She put on her glasses and pulled up the hood on her coat. Finally, she walked over to the bus shelter, sat on it's bench and perused the local map she had found in the Post Office. Having got her bearings, she set off towards Simon's Fel.

Chapter Thirty-Eight

"OK, Lucy, I'll be there in twenty minutes." James jumped up from his chair quickly to change into smarter clothes and then he went off to The Tavern.

Lucy had phoned to say that Sandra was unwell and they wondered if he could help them out. James was more than happy to do so as it meant extra money for him! He had gone out for the day yesterday, taking photos of the local area and sketching anything that appealed to him; he wanted to build up his portfolio in readiness for his plans to publish. He had planned to go out again, but that could wait for another day. He was glad to earn extra money from The Tavern!

It had been a few days since he'd seen Melissa, and so had wondered if she was still at the pub. When he arrived, was soon informed by Lucy that Melissa was still there as she had decided to stay until tomorrow, and there were two other couples who had booked to stay who were due in later today. She left James in charge of the bar and went off to the office to continue working.

Michael came in from the kitchen to say hello and to thank James for stepping in at short notice to help them out.

Customers were arriving, so James set to work immediately as it had suddenly become very busy. It was lunchtime, and there were many people who wanted food as well as drinks. Before he knew it, it was mid-afternoon, and the bar was nearly empty. Most diners had left the dining room, so at last James had time to tidy up the bar and the tables. The door then opened, and the two couples who had booked to stay arrived together. James soon had them settled, gave them their room keys and booked them a table for dinner that night.

Michael came into the bar with sandwiches and coffee for James. "Sit down and take five minutes to have a rest – you deserve it." He smiled and left James sitting at a table enjoying his well-earned break.

Just then, the door opened, James jumped up from his seat and went back to the bar in readiness to serve the customer. To his surprise, it was Melissa facing him.

"Hello, how are you? Are you enjoying your stay? May I get you…?" James's voice trailed off as he saw Melissa scowling at him.

She quickly realised that he was looking at her, waiting for an answer to his questions. Forcing a smile on her face, she apologised, "I'm sorry; I couldn't find my key. I'd like a large glass of dry white wine, please. It's very quiet in here today."

James poured the glass of wine and handed it to Melissa. "It's been really busy. I hope your day has been enjoyable so far." He was taken aback somewhat at her sudden change of mood and was wondering what had made her scowl like that. Surely a missing key was not that important? After all, they had duplicates in the office.

It seemed as though he may have misjudged her, as she sat down at the bar, and they had a pleasant and quite lively conversation.

Finally, Melissa stood up and stated she was going to her room as she needed to pack because she was leaving in the morning. James quickly made arrangements to meet her that evening in The Tavern after she'd had dinner. She seemed pleased by the invitation and agreed to meet him. She went off to her room, and James finished his shift as Lucy was taking over to cover for Sandra that evening, so he now had time for a couple of hours' work on his project before he was going to meet up with Melissa.

As he got home, he went to find Felicity to tell her that he would be going out that evening, but he would join them all for dinner first. He went off whistling happily; he'd had such a good day, and hopefully, he would find out more about Melissa tonight. She intrigued him, and he was looking forward to getting to know her.

Chapter Thirty-Nine

Melissa was very thoughtful as she packed her suitcase in readiness for her departure the next day. She had made all sorts of discreet enquiries about the cottage, such as who it belonged to and who lived there. She spent time in the library and the Church, going around the churchyard itself and looking at the gravestones, searching for any names that might give her any clue about the original owners of the cottage. She made sure she gave the impression that she was a tourist, taking as many pictures as she could, most of which were going to be deleted.

Now, though, she'd met someone who lived here! She did vaguely remember meeting him in London and also at Bristol Uni, and she soon realised he could prove very useful in her quest, so she resolved to nurture a friendship to that end. She smiled to herself, happy that she had a plan in place to find out all she could in order to gain the property that she considered to be hers by right.

James proved to be good company: he was pleasant, charming and thoughtful. He was enjoying Melissa's company too, although she could sometimes be quite distant and cold. He decided it was because she was alone and had no family; she'd told him that much. He was returning with some more drinks from the bar when he noticed his father and Abe walking into the pub. He placed the drinks on the table, excused himself to Melissa, and went over to greet his Dad and Abe. "Come over, Dad, and meet Melissa. She's staying here and is at the same University as me."

"OK, Son; Abe and I will get our drinks and then we'll be along to say hello." Simon smiled at James and went to join Abe at the bar. Both men were surprised that James was with someone, as he'd never shown any interest in women before!

James went back to Melissa and told her his Dad was going to come over to meet her. She nodded, making small talk with James until his Father appeared. Melissa watched as the two men approached; her first instinct was incredulity. It couldn't be! That man looked so much like the man who had defiled her Mother! She pulled herself together and greeted them with a neutral expression.

James stood up and introduced Simon and Abe to Melissa. She greeted them politely, all the while thinking fast as she realised there was more to know, more to find out; she must read her mother's papers again and scrutinise them very carefully.

Meanwhile, Simon had taken an immediate

dislike to the young woman. But why? What was it about her that made him feel like that? Abe felt Simon's discomfort and also wondered why. However, he smiled and tried his best to cover over any awkward feelings. He soon steered Simon away, simply saying that they had business to discuss. Simon barely acknowledged Melissa; he couldn't understand his instant dislike – people didn't normally affect him like that. James too had noticed his Father's odd behaviour; he would definitely speak to him later.

Melissa didn't seem to notice anything strange but shortly afterwards she said goodnight to James and that she would see him when they got back to University, then went off to her room. James was left feeling that he had somehow missed something, but was at a loss to know what! He sighed and went to join his Dad and Abe, who were laughing together, obviously enjoying their evening. They motioned for James to sit down and join them. Nothing was said about Melissa or the tension of the meeting. The three of them enjoyed the rest of the evening.

The only mention of Melissa came from Simon. Abe had gone to get some drinks, and Simon turned to James. "Sorry, Son, I hope I didn't seem rude, but Melissa reminded me of someone – though I can't remember who! No matter; it's not important."

James smiled at his Dad, glad it was cleared up. However, Simon didn't say that he'd explained to Abe his discomfiture and the reasons for it. Abe had said he would help him work it all out. Both Abe and

Simon would investigate first and then tell their wives, but Simon once again had the sinking feeling that the James family was not finished with them yet.

Chapter Forty

Melissa arrived home angry, frustrated and intent on wreaking vengeance on the James family. The first thing she did on getting home was to pour herself a large glass of wine. She calmed down and looked around the flat. It was now just as she wanted it: modern, bright and with all the appliances built in. A satisfied smile spread across her face; there would be more to come, she was sure. She poured another glass of wine and decided to look carefully at her Mother's papers again.

Gathering all the papers together, she sat at the table, phoned for a takeaway and started meticulously studying the papers. Hours later, she checked the notes she'd made. It was enlightening to see what she had unearthed. It was just the outcome she'd hoped for! It was late, and she hadn't unpacked from her trip, so she would leave that until tomorrow. What she needed right now was a long soak in the bath, plus a glass of champagne to celebrate her forthcoming good fortune.

The next day, Melissa nursed a hangover, but she gritted her teeth and planned the few days she had remaining before being back at Uni. Fortunately she had worked very hard during the last term so she had little to do regarding her law course. Consequently, she concentrated on finding out all she could about the James family. She searched the internet for birth, marriage and death records. Census papers, local and parish records. It took her three days to compile a family tree of the James family – or at least enough of one to give her all the information she felt she needed. At last, at last! She had something that could reward her with what she wanted. She danced around the flat, then decided to take herself out for dinner. While she was at the restaurant, she would make plans for the changes she wanted to make at the block of flats; she was, after all, the freeholder.

Two days later, she was back at Bristol University, wondering just how she could get James Grantley to bend to her will.

Back in Little Trenchard, Simon and Abe were making their own plans. Simon had told Abe all about his own life, the ups and downs, and how he had discovered the truth about his own lost relatives. The path towards finding out the full extent of the James family was not straightforward as Melissa's had been. It took them months to sort it all out, and it was nearly Christmas again before they found all the information. When they had the final information, both of them feared the worst.

Chapter Forty-One

Felicity thought James would tell her about Melissa, but he'd left to go back to Bristol before she knew anything. Simon had mentioned that he and Abe had met her in The Tavern, but she'd left the next day. That was all he said, and Abe did not expand on that, so she just thought it was all of no importance.

The children were all growing up and at school or nursery. Bella and Stan were happy at Pops' Place, and Dave and Vanessa had settled into Abe and Jeannie's extension. Seb came home from New Zealand for three weeks and brought his flat mate Bryan too. Janine mooched about the whole time they were there, declaring to anyone who would listen that she was going to marry Bryan.

Justin came to Little Trenchard with his girlfriend, who was his fiancée by the time they went back. It was another excuse for a party, which was enjoyed by everyone. Most of the village went along, thrilled that, at last, Justin had found his soul mate. Firm promises were made that all the family would go to New Zealand for the wedding! They were all so surprised when Justin and Carla announced that they wanted to get married in Little Trenchard. Their minds were made up; they were adamant! Lucy wrote to Carla's parents, inviting them to stay in the bed and breakfast for however long they wanted. This letter started off a friendship that became everlasting.

---
*

James didn't see much of Melissa when he first got back to Uni, mostly because they were both entrenched in their studies towards their law degrees. After some while, James found himself bumping into Melissa frequently, so much so that, one day, he stopped her purposefully and arranged to take her out to dinner. She accepted with a smile, and after that, they went out regularly, except weekends as he always went home to Little Trenchard.

Inevitably, James eventually called his Mum and said he would be bringing a friend with him who would stay at The Tavern. He gave no details except to say it was "a friend from Uni". When telling Simon this, Felicity noticed he had gone pale, but Simon explained it away by saying that he was tired.

---
*

The weekend arrived. James dropped Melissa at the The Tavern to book into her room then went home to his cabin. Nothing much was said except for Simon commenting that he should be careful and to not forget that he was deep into his studies for a degree. Felicity had raised her eyebrows at this remark.

James had laughed it off, remarking on how could he forget? As far as he was concerned, nothing was going to stop from him attaining his goal.

They hardly saw anything of Melissa; James was working at The Tavern, and Melissa went off in her own car, although where she went, no one knew. She took great delight in nosing around, taking pictures of the children, Simon and Felicity, together with anyone else who could be of use one way or another in her scheme. She made friends with Janine, subtly and quietly – almost unobtrusively. Janine was very informative without knowing she was being so. Any question asked of her were done in such a way that it seemed so innocent. Melissa was a very clever and devious woman. She never got too close to either Felicity or Jeannie, as she recognised that both women could catch her out. The only person she tried to get close to was Bella, but she immediately felt uncomfortable in her presence so she therefore avoided the young Mum at all costs.

Bella never said anything to her mother or Felicity – after all, she had Matthew and Stan to care for (*and maybe another baby soon?*)! She enjoyed being a Mum, and although she missed her work, she could go back to it again later. She smiled to herself; she couldn't imagine for one moment Melissa with a baby! Another thought came to her: she hoped James didn't get too fond of Melissa, but then felt she was being daft, as after all, surely he wouldn't be that foolish?

$$*$$

Suddenly, Christmas was upon them. James was due home the next day, and the children finished school the following week. Jeannie and Felicity had stopped their classes at The Hobby Loft until mid-January; they wanted to refresh the itinerary and try some of the new ideas their current attendees had suggested. Abe had found he was good as a landlord and had started his own business, which he worked at three times a week. He had his own rental property portfolio: he'd taken over the rental duties for Pops' Place from Lucy and Michael, and he currently had two more properties on his books, with a third pending. He'd decided the maximum he would have in his portfolio would be ten, and having ready-made builders and a handyman he could use – by way of Stan, Dave and Simon – made this manageable.

As usual, everyone in the village was looking forward to Christmas.

Seb and his flatmate were staying in New Zealand and saving to come home when Justin and Carla got married, although no news of an actual date yet!

Felicity was wondering about James and Melissa, but she thought it better to say nothing unless James did. Simon had been strangely reticent when she mentioned Melissa, so she'd dropped the subject as she imagined she would know soon enough.

As for Melissa, she'd made her own plans. Using a different name, she'd booked a room at the small but very comfortable hotel in Middle Trenchard. She wanted to arrive incognito, so she'd told James that she would be staying at home and studying.

He would be very surprised to see her, and even more surprised when she revealed her plans, little by little, and then it would be too late! She laughed out loud; what fun it was going to be!

Chapter Forty-Two

Lucy and Michael invited their closest family and friends to a buffet supper at The Tavern on Boxing Day evening. Stan and Bella, along with Matthew, Dave and Vanessa, together with their respective babies, were invited too as part of the growing family. Everyone was enjoying themselves as the telephone rang. Lucy went off to answer it and came back a few minutes later, smiling hugely.

She went straight to Michael, who immediately shouted for silence, "Justin and Carla are getting married next year in August and her parents are coming too and staying here with us," he announced. He grabbed Lucy, swung her around, kissed her and went off to open a bottle of champagne.

Everybody started talking at once, thinking how good it would be to have the wedding in the village. There was much speculation on how it would be arranged, who would be there, who the bridesmaids would be and who the best man would be.

So much was being talked about that James missed a call on his mobile. He heard a ping heralding a text message, so he went outside to read it. Astonished and surprised, he found it was from Melissa, simply asking if he could call her. Immediately, he rang her back. She explained that she wanted to meet him tomorrow, and told him where she was staying. He agreed, saying he would see her at 11am and they could perhaps have lunch at her hotel. He was even more surprised to learn that she was in the next village. He started to ask her why she hadn't told him she was staying nearby, but she cut him short and just said, "Looking forward to seeing you tomorrow! Take care, bye." She then rang off, leaving James staring at his phone, completely stunned!

He wandered slowly back into The Tavern, having quickly decided to say nothing to his parents about Melissa; he would wait until he'd seen her. He was smiling, though, excited at the thought she'd come to see him. No one questioned him as to why he'd gone outside; they were all too busy discussing Justin's news.

*

During the next few days, things became a lot clearer. Lucy and Michael had a long chat with Justin and Carla to discuss their plans, and they arranged for her parents – Gino and Marie – to stay at The Tavern.

Justin said, "We all plan to come over together and stay for six weeks to arrange the wedding, which will be in the last week of August. I would like Simon to be my best man, and Carla has asked if Janine would be her bridesmaid as she's an only child. She has no aunts or uncles, and most of her friends are unlikely to be able to take that amount of time off work, plus a lot of our friends are married and have children too." Justin stopped at this point, then he added. "The people who are most important to me are in Little Trenchard, I want you to celebrate our special day with us."

He then spoke to Simon and Janine (Lucy had asked them to be there at The Tavern for the planned phone call). Simon was honoured and thrilled to be asked, and Janine was so excited that she could barely speak.

---
*

No one had noticed that James was absent; he often disappeared to go out sketching and taking photos, so it wasn't unusual. When he finally called into the cottage, it was a few days after the initial call from Melissa. "Mum, Dad, I've been seeing Melissa; she's been staying in Middle Trenchard. I'd like to invite her here tonight to introduce her to you, as she's going back to Bristol tomorrow. Would that be OK? We won't need dinner as we're eating at the hotel; it's just a drink to say hello."

Felicity felt Simon stiffen beside her, she looked quickly at him, but he was smiling, his facial expression not giving anything away.

"That's fine, James; is about 8.30pm OK for you?" Simon queried.

"Thanks, Dad; that's great." He smiled at his parents and went off whistling.

Felicity declared, "That's a surprise. I didn't know he knew her that well." She turned to Simon, but the expression on his face told her he wasn't pleased at all with this turn of events "He's old enough to choose his own friends Simon; we can't choose them for him. Coffee or something stronger?" she asked as she got up.

"Something a lot stronger," he said.

She raised her eyebrows at this, but forbore to answer. Simon resolved to speak to Abe in the morning; they must get together and find out if there was anything they should know about Melissa.

*

The next evening, 8.30pm came and went. It was approaching 9.15pm when James tapped at the front door and came in, followed by Melissa. He was smiling as he introduced her and apologised for being late. Conversation was subdued; Melissa was intent on making Simon and Felicity know of her superiority in her year at Uni and how she had her ambitions to become a barrister. It was apparent to them both that nothing would be allowed to get in her way. Felicity couldn't quite understand her relationship with James. He seemed to be a bit in awe of her, and was listening intently to everything she said.

They only stayed for about an hour, then left. James was going to drive her back to the hotel, but as Felicity shut the curtains in her sitting room, she noticed James's car in the drive, he could not possibly have driven to Middle Trenchard in that time, as they only left about ten minutes ago. She checked her watch and looked out of the window again. There was nothing to see and the cabin was in darkness, but the car was still there.

When Felicity got up the next morning, she saw Melissa get into the passenger seat of James's car, her immediate thought and her feelings were that he'd picked the wrong girl.

Chapter Forty-Three

James didn't see much of his parents over the next few days as he was either working at The Tavern or out sketching and taking photos. When he finally called in at the cottage, he found his Mum in the kitchen, baking as usual.

"Have some tea, James; I've just made one for myself," she offered.

He sat down and asked, "Where are all the children? Is Dad OK?"

"The children have gone to Jeannie's for the afternoon. She invited them all as Bella and Vanessa are going to be there with their babies. Your Dad's tinkering with Ray's old car; I think he's nearly finished the restoration."

James nodded. "I'll be going back to University next week, but I shall be leaving a couple of days earlier than I originally planned as I've arranged to see Melissa on my way back."

Felicity felt he had stated this in a defiant tone, especially as she got the impression he was looking for some sort of reaction from her. However, she just said, "That's great; we're pleased you've made friends at University," while keeping her back to him, mostly to cover up the look of dismay on her face at James's announcement. Then, having managed to summon up a smile, she turned towards James. "We'll miss you, but I'm sure you'll be back soon. Dad will be pleased to have your opinion on the car."

She turned away from James to give the impression she was continuing with her baking, then she heard the door close behind him. She sat down, picked up her cup of tea and hoped James had taken the hint and gone to see his Father. He was now old enough to choose his own friends; however, she was very worried about his liaison with Melissa. She and Simon must have a serious talk!

*

The door swung open, and Simon and James came in together, laughing happily.

"We've finished it, Mum; Dad's taking me out for a ride in it, so we'll be about an hour." He turned to Felicity, still smiling. "I'm off to get my jacket, Mum; see you outside, Dad."

Felicity quickly looked at Simon. "Did he tell you about Melissa?"

"Yes, he did; we'll talk later, but right now we're off in Ray's old car."

Simon didn't mention Melissa whilst they were out; he wanted to just enjoy his time with James. They had a good run in the car, which was going well. Simon was thrilled that, at long last, it had been restored back to its former glory.

---
*

James joined them all at dinner that evening; nothing was mentioned about him seeing Melissa, as neither Simon nor Felicity wanted to spoil the evening because James was leaving for Uni the following morning.

---
*

They all waved James off after breakfast, and it was much later in the day before Simon and Felicity managed to get a chance to discuss Melissa.

"I'm really worried," Simon began, "There's something about Melissa that I don't understand and, frankly, I don't like. I'll speak to Abe and see if he's managed to find anything out about her background. I have the feeling that there's something unsavoury about her."

Felicity looked at Simon with concern. "You seem quite upset about her, but we must let James choose his own friends. Although, I admit, I too don't care much for her. One minute she seems quite friendly, then she turns and appears to dislike us, yet she hardly knows us!"

Simon thought for a while, then put his arm around Felicity to give her some reassurance,

"Don't fret too much, darling. I'll have a long talk with Abe; he volunteered to help me, so we'll do all we can to see if our worries are unfounded. I have an idea that we should also recheck the validity of our ownership of the cottage, to ensure we're legally protected from every angle. Ray told us that there was no problem, but I want to be sure!"

He stopped speaking and Felicity settled comfortably into his arms. Surely nothing could be wrong? But she would let Simon check everything with Abe's help. However, she resolved privately to find out for herself exactly what it was about Melissa that concerned her so much. Just how she would do that she wasn't sure, but do it she must.

Chapter Forty-Four

Meanwhile, Melissa put her own plans into place and congratulated herself that she had James hooked!

Chuckling to herself, she planned to spend the time before James arrived going over the papers again and studying the James' family tree. She was almost sure she had a full picture now and was just waiting for the right time to instigate her plans. She'd never had much affection for her Mother, but just maybe, her Mother's association with Geoffrey James could reap the benefits she felt should be hers, after all! She danced round the room with excitement and then opened a bottle of champagne in celebration.

—
*

James left Little Trenchard feeling somewhat disheartened. He wasn't sure exactly why he felt that way. It was something he couldn't quite put his finger on, and he felt it was something to do with his parents and Melissa, but what? They'd parted on good terms, but the more he thought about it, the more he was convinced it was what they *didn't* say, not anything they *did* say! He sighed heavily and stopped thinking about it. He was on his way to meet Melissa, so maybe she would know something. He turned the radio on, as he decided to enjoy the journey, and he settled his thoughts on the work he needed to complete next term.

*

Back in Cornwall, Lucy and Michael started on the plans for Justin and Carla's wedding in August. Jeannie had offered Carla a room to stay in before the wedding, and she made a point of mentioning that it had a double bed and its own en suite, knowing that they lived together most of the time in New Zealand. Carla's parents were very pleased to hear this, as they'd been concerned that Jason would be unhappy being alone at The Tavern with both sets of parents.

*

Felicity and Jeannie were busy with their classes at The Hobby Loft and had encouraged their students to help them make room and table decorations, table mats, and serviettes for the wedding day. What with the children now all being at school and nursery, it meant that they had more time to concentrate on the celebrations to come! Felicity had racked her brains on how to find out all she could about Melissa, but couldn't fathom where to start, so decided to wait to see what Simon and Abe could discover first.

Exciting news from Bella put things on hold for a while, with Stan having proudly announced that they were having another baby. They had been speaking to the Carlyons (who had bought the estate agency from Ray), as they had decided to sell up and retire! Apparently, years ago, the office and the flat had originally all been one large property that had been split into the estate agency and the upstairs flat. So the Carlyons had asked Stan and Bella if they would like to purchase it and turn it back into a house again. Stan had been in touch with the Council's planning department, which had no objections to it being returned to its original use.

Abe and Jeannie were thrilled at the news – both at another grandchild and the prospect of a house for their family. Bella and Jeannie cried happy tears, and Abe offered to help with the plans and alterations. It was going to be a big job, but with their help – plus assistance from Dave and Simon – it would be an exciting project. Lucy and Michael were overjoyed and immediately agreed that Stan and Bella could buy the flat to complete the whole purchase. Michael, Stan and the Carlyons would meet with the solicitor and the mortgage broker (known to the Carlyons through their business) in the coming days to sort out all the legalities and paperwork. It was a lot to take in all at once, but it was also another excuse for an impromptu party at The Tavern!

*

A few days later, Simon was with Abe, discussing the plans for doing the outside work needed at Pops' Place, when his mobile phone pinged, telling him a message had come through. It was from the solicitor he had seen in London after his Father died, asking him to call urgently.

He went quickly to his landline and dialled the solicitor's number; he never thought he would need to contact him again.

The solicitor answered straightaway. "Good afternoon, Mr Grantley; I thought you should know immediately that I have received some paperwork that claims your house, Simon's Fel, is in dispute regarding your ownership of it. I need to authenticate the details first and then I will send you my findings in due course."

Completely stunned and shaken, Simon's mind went abruptly into a whirl from the information he had just received. He took a deep breath to steady himself.

"Mr Gregson, thank you for the information. Please let me know the outcome of your investigations as soon as possible. For your records and information, you should be aware that I'm not the legal owner of Simon's Fel. My wife is the sole owner."

He broke off the conversation, still shaking with shock.

Abe, being in the room with him, went over to him quickly; Simon looked as though he might pass out – the colour had drained from his face. "What is it, Simon? Do you need help?"

"I'll be OK, Abe, just give me a new moments."

Abe waited for Simon to settle himself.

Simon finally looked at Abe. "Somebody in that bloody awful family of mine has made a claim on Simon's Fell. It will never be theirs, Abe; never, whoever it is!"

Chapter Forty-Five

Shocked by what Simon had said, Abe was speechless; he couldn't think of anything to say. He waited, completely at a loss, until Simon felt able to speak.

"Abe, it's going to be difficult, but will you keep this quiet for the moment? I need time to think and time to plan what to do. I'll need your help more than ever now. We have to find out urgently all there is to know about the James family. Even if we have to go to London, we must." Simon stopped speaking, frowned and then went on, "I don't want Felicity to know anything at the moment, as I don't want her worrying and getting upset just yet. Let's just do this together as quickly as we can. I really need your help with this." Simon put his head in his hands, trying not to breakdown as he needed to hold himself together for now.

"Simon," Abe said, "Simon, listen to me. Jeannie and Felicity will be back soon. I'll arrange for us to go to London on the pretence of looking for special materials for the alterations at Pops' Place. We'll go on Monday, which is in three days' time, and if we go in Ray's car, we can tell Jeannie and Felicity that we want to take it for a good run. This will be our best opportunity, so in the meantime, make sure you have all the paperwork together that you'll need to take with us, and I'll arrange somewhere for us to stay. Just hold yourself together for the next few days; however, let Felicity know when she gets home that we're going away. I'll call in and see you later with the details for the trip."He hugged Simon, smiled at him and rushed out.

There were a few things Abe needed to find out and quickly. He went straight to The Tavern, knowing that Michael would be there. He dashed through the back door into the kitchen, startling Michael, who was busy peeling vegetables. "Can I look at your reservation books, please, Michael? It's really important as I need the one that goes back to when Felicity first came here?"

Michael stopped what he was doing and went across to the office, then having searched through the books, he passed one over to Abe. "I think this is the one you may want."

Abe took it from him and then leafed through the pages quickly."Yes, this is it; thanks."

Michael watched as Abe grabbed a pad and pen off the side of the desk and made a few notes.

Abe then tore the page with his notes on from the pad, handing back the reservation book and said, "Thanks, Michael. I'll explain everything when I can, but for now, please bear with me and don't tell anyone

I was here asking you for this. If anyone should, then just make something up if necessary."

Abe then dashed off, leaving Michael wondering what on earth he was up to, but he shrugged his shoulders and put it to one side; he still had loads of work to do.

---
*

Simon was very quiet but told Felicity that he'd been with Abe all afternoon and now had a headache from sorting out the list of materials they felt were required for the renovations. Oh, and he and Abe would need to go to London soon to source certain materials, and that Abe was coming round later with the details for that trip.

Felicity accepted this explanation, thinking only that Simon should slow down a bit and to consider that Abe was somewhat older than him.

---
*

Jeannie was more perceptive; she'd frowned at Abe's explanation as to why they were going away together, even if they were taking Ray's car. She didn't believe he was telling her the whole story, but she knew he would tell her when he could. She watched him closely all evening and was aware he had something on his mind.

He was very attentive and aware of the way she was looking at him, and finally, he said to her, "I'll let you know what's concerning me as soon as I can, but for now, just trust me that it isn't me who has the problem, but someone very close to both of us. Please say nothing to anyone at the moment." He kissed her tenderly and went into the study.

She trusted his judgement and would do as he asked, wait for now and to not worry. Three days later, Abe and Simon went off in Ray's car, waving madly as they disappeared round the bend.

Felicity went off to The Hobby Loft with Jeannie, chatting together amiably about the progress they were making for the wedding party. It was going really well, and their students had been so helpful. As they neared their destination, Felicity turned to Jeannie and said, "Has Abe been OK lately? Simon has been very quiet, and I was just wondering if all was well with you?"

Jeannie quickly reassured her friend that all was well and it was nothing more than planning the renovations for Pops' Place that was concerning them – and the new baby too, of course.

Felicity immediately changed the subject to the birth of the baby and said jokingly that she wished it were her who was pregnant! Jeannie breathed a sigh of relief, at least she had avoided any awkward questions.

As they went into The Hobby Loft, Jeannie uttered a silent prayer, hoping that Abe and Simon would be home soon.

Chapter Forty-Six

Abe directed Simon towards the row of town houses where Felicity had lived with Gordon James. It was a difficult visit for Simon, but Abe had just said that it was an absolute necessity. It was quite late when they arrived. A tall, slim man in a business suit was handing over the keys to his car to a valet for it to be put away when Abe strode up to him, smiling politely.

"Good evening, do you live in this building by any chance? I'm trying to trace someone?" Abe enquired.

"Excuse me, but who are you? And who are you looking for?" the man replied.

Abe smiled again and handed over his business card, which showed the name of his rental business. "I'm Mr Bresland, and I'm trying to trace Felicity Huntley?"

The young man put out his hand to Abe in greeting. "I'm Alexander Gossington; I bought my town house from Mrs Huntley many years ago now. A very good investment, I must say."

Bingo! thought Abe. "Would you have a few moments spare, Mr Gossington?"

"Please, come in," he said to Abe, "I would be happy to be of help, if I can."

It was about forty minutes later that Simon saw Abe taking his leave from the town house. Abe got back to the car and told Simon that he had learnt a fair bit about Felicity and Gordon James. First, though, he decided they needed to book into a Travelodge and to find somewhere to eat and drink.

Half an hour later, they were in a local pub, nursing beers and perusing the menu. After having ordered their food, Abe related to Simon what he had learnt from Alexander Gossington.

The marriage hadn't been a happy one. Apparently, Gordon James had ruled the roost and hadn't allowed Felicity to work; he'd just expected her to be at his beck and call at all times and to be the trophy wife on his arm. Seemingly, her mother had encouraged this and agreed with everything that Gordon had decreed. Simon had learnt certain things from Felicity, but he hadn't been aware of just how cruel Gordon James was or just how much she had suffered with him.

Abe stopped talking as their food had arrived; they chatted as they ate, but Simon's mind was thinking of Felicity and why he was so unsure about their future. They settled down with a coffee after their meal, and Abe continued his tale. Apparently, when Felicity had left and sold her house, Alexander Gossington had tried to find her, as he'd found several items in the loft that he wanted to return to her. Abe had asked

Alexander if he still had these items, and if so, could he take them to give to Felicity, which would save him the trouble of sending them? Alexander readily agreed to this and arranged for Abe to pick them up from his house early the next morning. He explained that the papers were still packed in two boxes, just as they had been left, and that he just had to get them down out of the loft.

Alexander had then gone on to say that his search to find Felicity had only resulted in him tracing her mother and the James family. In doing this, he discovered that Gordon James's father had an illegitimate daughter who was two years older than James – and her name was Melissa.

Chapter Forty-Seven

Stunned and shocked, Simon's face drained of colour. His mind was in a whirl; he couldn't think straight when he realised that she was indeed his half-sister! They had the same father!

"Abe, we have to go home and sort this out," he stated. "She's going to try to take our home, I just know she is. I've never trusted her, but now she has contrived a relationship with James! She's his aunt or something – I have to work it out properly – but she is a threat to us, and James in particular. What if she becomes pregnant? I feel sure their relationship may have gone that far!" Simon slumped back in his chair.

Abe tried to reason with him by saying that they would leave soon, but they needed another day. He phoned Jeannie and gave her a brief explanation of their findings. He explained that they would clarify everything fully when they got home, but in the meantime asked her to look after Felicity and to say nothing to James if he should come home.

Simon rang Felicity, but he told her only that he and Abe would be home soon – in the next day or two, at least – and they'd found out most of what they needed. He had ended their phone call very reluctantly, as he was missing her so much, but he realised Abe had been right. Apart from finding out about suppliers for the renovations (which they'd almost forgotten about), there were Felicity's belongings to collect and a few things that Abe wanted to ask the solicitor who had dealt with the Will of Simon's father.

Puzzled, Simon asked Abe what he was hoping to find out.

"I'm not sure, Simon, but I just feel that there's something not quite right with the whole story, perhaps with the family solicitor representing the James family and also the family firm, as there must be something they must know. Even if it takes us a couple more days, it could be worth it."

Simon was not at all pleased that their return home would be delayed, but he agreed that it made sense to stay a day or two longer.

*

The next morning, Abe went out to meet Alexander Gossington at the town house, leaving Simon to collate all the papers they'd brought with them relating to Pops' Place.

Alexander was waiting for Abe as he drove up to the town house, all of Felicity's belongings were stacked in the hallway. "Please come in, Mr Bresland.

I have everything ready for you. I forgot to mention yesterday that I'd received two phone calls from a Miss Cartwright, asking for information regarding Gordon James and where he was. I had dismissed them as just someone being nosy and therefore ignored them. However, I regret that I only remembered this morning that Gordon James was the name of Mrs Huntley's late husband – plus, it was quite some time ago that I'd received those phone calls."

"Thank you for the information," Abe said, "It could be of some use, and I'm grateful to you for keeping the items for Mrs Grantley. I'll make sure she gets them." Abe smiled and took his leave of Alexander Gossington and went back to the hotel to pick up Simon.

Having done so, they set off to visit a few builders' merchants and suppliers, hoping to find bricks, internal doors, flooring and bathroom fitments within the scope of Bella and Stan's budget. As the day went on Abe was pleased to see Simon becoming calmer and more relaxed. Giving him something time-consuming and important to do had stopped him from becoming morose and withdrawn.

Abe had then arranged a meeting with the solicitor for late afternoon. Mr Gregson would be expecting them, especially after Simon's call with him regarding the ownership of Simon's Fel, as he'd started to tell Simon there was currently a dispute about the legality of their ownership of the cottage.

Having arrived at the solicitor's office Simon began "This matter has necessitated my visit making it imperative that we speak to you. I need to know if the question of ownership is from a young lady who's known as Melissa Cartwright?"

Abe looked at Simon, astonished that he'd immediately asked this direct question of the solicitor.

Mr Gregson was taken aback by Simon's question, which took him a few moments to answer. "Mr Grantley, it would be breaching professional etiquette to give out details of our clients to other people; however, given that you are a part of the same family you are therefore entitled to know that we have heard from a Miss Cartwright and are currently investigating the validity of her claim with regard to your late father's estate. Furthermore, all I can say at this point is that our enquiries are at an early stage and we cannot give you any further information."

Simon sighed and then asked that he be informed of any developments that may arise from this situation. He left all his contact details and began to rise from his seat in readiness to leave with Abe.

As he did so, Mr Gregson stated, "I can tell you that our preliminary enquiries show that, from the terms of your father's Will, Miss Cartwright would appear to have no claim. However, in law, we do have to explore all possibilities to confirm that this is correct so as to be in a position to legally dismiss her claim."

Simon and Abe left, not as worried as they had been, but Simon vowed that, when he got home, he would get all the papers regarding his ownership of the cottage triple checked .He was sure in his own heart that his good friend Ray Luxton had not let him down.

Chapter Forty-Eight

James hadn't been home for a while as he was studying very hard and also trying to complete his book of sketches and photographs, but he was in regular contact with his parents. Plus, he'd been in touch with Michael to ask if he could keep his job at The Tavern open for him so that he'd have work during University breaks. He was fully aware why he was working so hard. It was mostly to stop him thinking about Melissa!

He had gone to stay with her at her flat on his way back to University, but he'd immediately felt uncomfortable when he'd arrived. It was so cold and unwelcoming; there was no soul in the place. It was so minimalistic and stark in its decor. His first instinct was to ask himself, "What am I doing here?"

Melissa had greeted him at the door, looking very pleased with herself, which made James wonder what could have happened to give him the impression that she was looking smug.

Suddenly, the thought had come to him that he was the fly and she was a spider weaving a web, but he was at a loss as to how to deal with this situation. To cover his discomfiture, he had smiled and accepted the drink she offered him. All this happened within a couple of minutes, but he had to work out how he could get away. Fortunately, he'd left his bags in his car, so he had no reason to stay.

Melissa didn't appear to notice any problem with James, as he was polite, answering her questions and chatting as he would with any other person in his acquaintance. She had cooked a pleasant meal, but James had beenfully aware that it had not been prepared by her! It was probably M & S, if not from there, then possibly Fortnum & Mason.

As the evening drew on, James became more aware that Melissa was slowly becoming drunk. She was flirting with him and trying to encourage him to drink more and more, making him feel even more uncomfortable than he was already.

Finally, she stood up and said, "I'm just going to change into something more comfortable."

James took his chance. "Please don't bother; I have to go, but thanks for a very nice dinner." He put down his half-empty glass, and gave her a peck on the cheek then went.

Once outside her flat, he found that he was shaking, but was pleased and relieved that he'd got away.

Since that evening, he hadn't contacted her again, but she had tried to call him several times. He'd blocked her from his mobile, although he'd mainly done that purely to help him with his studies so he could concentrate without so many interruptions. He'd also managed to avoid her at University by immersing himself in his lecture and study groups.

It had been a few weeks since he'd visited his parents, and it was time he went home to rest a little and to have some good home cooking. However, he also realised that he needed to apologise to his parents about Melissa.

Chapter Forty-Nine

Simon drove home, whilst Abe was snoozing quietly beside him. He had a great deal to think about; however, by the time they were home, his mind had cleared, and he was looking forward to seeing the family. Abe too was eager to get home to Jeannie and Janine – and, of course, Bella, Stan and Matthew; plus, it wouldn't be long before Seb was with them from New Zealand.

The two men arrived home in a buoyant mood and were greeted with great excitement from everyone. Felicity and Jeannie had made a huge pot of spaghetti bolognese, having decided they should all eat supper together. Once they'd all eaten, Abe, Jeannie and Janine finally went home, happy to be together again.

Felicity put the children to bed and joined Simon for a welcome home drink.

Settling down to tell Felicity all about their trip, Simon started from the beginning by describing what they learnt from Alexander Gossington. He had just got up to refill their glasses when the phone rang.

"Hi Dad, just a quick call as the battery's running out. I'll be with you late on Friday. Love you all!" The phone went dead.

Simon stood staring at Felicity, who was looking back at him as he slowly said to her, "James is coming home on Friday night."

Felicity sprang to her feet. "Ah! That's great; it feels as if he's been away for ages!"

Crushing Felicity to him, he kissed her, then went out into the kitchen to replenish their glasses. On returning and sitting back down next to her, he smiled and said, "It will be great to see him again; I've missed him."

Felicity cuddled up close to him on the sofa. "I think we've all missed him – the kids too! I just hope he doesn't bring that Melissa."

That was Simon's opening, so he carried on with the story, telling her everything – including the news from the solicitor.

Simon stood up again and turned to Felicity. "I just don't think James would bring her here again, and although she has more knowledge than James, she's got nil common sense! Anyway, we can ask him on Friday. Come on, I'm really tired. It's been a busy few days, and we have lots to plan tomorrow."

*

The following morning, Abe called round to pick up Simon. They were off to Pops' Place to discuss their ideas with Stan and Bella, so they could start planning the new layout of the building. The sale of the whole building was going through seamlessly, and Stan had received all the necessary planning permissions for them to proceed. They were all very aware that, with another baby on the way, they had to start work immediately.

Even the students at The Hobby Loft were keen to help. Alongside the preparations for Justin and Carla's wedding, they were also all eager to learn new skills to assist with curtains, cushions and even upholstery! It felt as though the whole village was involved.

Felicity had just stayed for the morning classes as she wanted to clean and air James's cabin, and to make it as welcoming as she could for his arrival later on. As she busily cleaned and shopped for essentials for him, she hoped fervently he would be on his own. After Simon had finished telling her about Melissa's background and everything that Abe and he had found out, she was very concerned and worried for James. She didn't want to contemplate the repercussions that could arise from a close relationship between James and Melissa. She sighed heavily and decided to leave worrying until after they'd spoken to James.

※

Simon and Abe had a very productive day with Bella and Stan, sorting out exactly what they wanted from their new home. There was a great deal to do, but everyone involved had been assigned their jobs and were all ready to start immediately – after the weekend, in fact! Abe was spending Saturday and Sunday with Stan to mark out the site, measure everything, ensure they'd ordered the scaffolding and confirm delivery dates. Abe was designated as the project manager, and had the hat to prove it!

*

That evening, Simon and Felicity fed the children and got them ready for bed, but they'd allowed them to wait up to see their big brother. They'd been so excited to see him when he arrived, that it took some time for them to quieten down and get them settled in bed.

It was late when James finally managed to sit down with his parents. He'd unpacked his luggage and freshened up in the cabin, before settling down to have something to eat.

He then began to tell his tale. "Before you say anything, Mum and Dad, I want to reassure you that nothing untoward happened between Melissa and me. At first, she wouldn't, and then when she decided the time was right, *I just couldn't*. By then, I'd realised I was uncomfortable being with her. I can't quite explain why, but she was getting quite drunk – which I now realise was something she often did – and I couldn't get away fast enough!" James stopped to have a drink and to eat some food.

Astonished, Simon and Felicity looked at each other and breathed a huge sigh of relief.

Simon broke the silence. "I'm glad to hear you had the sense to walk away, Son." He choked back tears of relief.

Felicity just smiled radiantly and refilled their glasses.

Chapter Fifty

James, Simon and Felicity talked late into the night, discussing between them everything involving the James family. There were no more secrets left between them, with their understanding about the family was complete. They discussed their futures and how to ensure they were all protected. James finally understood the animosity Simon had felt against James's choice of career and why there was so much anxiety involved over the ownership of the cottage.

After they had all gone to bed, James lay awake for a long while, working out how he could best help his parents achieve the security of Simon's Fel.

Felicity and Simon were exhausted as they fell into bed, too tired to discuss what had been said, except to say how thrilled they were to know that James had realised Melissa's true nature.

*

They were woken up early in the morning by three hungry children bouncing on their bed crying out, "Where's James? Where's James?"

Simon groaned, and Felicity climbed out of bed to shoo the children out, telling them as they all went downstairs that she would get them breakfast and they weren't to disturb James. But a few moments later, she was astonished to see James walk into the kitchen, fully dressed and asking if he could join in with the breakfast party.

Five minutes later, James had all of them listening to his stories as they ate, while Felicity went upstairs with a mug of coffee for Simon.

"James is entertaining the children and is going to get them all ready to go out with him to photograph the birds and bees, as he put it. So, it'll give us time to get up, sort ourselves out and put a plan in place to outwit Melissa. We must be prepared for when the solicitor calls us," Felicity declared.

Simon grunted a reply, and Felicity went off to prepare herself for a day of paperwork, smiling as she went; she was so happy to have all her family about her again.

Later that day, James went to see Michael at The Tavern wanting to say hello and also to ensure his job was still there for him for the next couple of months. Michael and Lucy were thrilled to see him and overjoyed that he would be there for the summer.

"We're going to be so busy," Lucy said. "Justin, Carla and her parents are coming from New Zealand on 10th July for the wedding on 14th August. When can you be here?"

"I finish at Uni on 7th July, so I can be here ready to work a couple of days later. Would that be OK?" James queried.

"Thank you so much, James; we'll be so thrilled to have you back here." Lucy hugged James, and Michael merely shook his hand off.

James stayed for a while, chatting to them and discussing what they would need him to do. He went away feeling more settled and happier than he had for some time.

When he got back to the cabin, after letting himself in and making a cup of coffee, he sat and thought hard about his future. He'd really enjoyed his time with his siblings, taking photos of them all and their antics with the birds and bees, which gave him the idea of making picture books of those photos for the children – could this be another career or way forward for the future? He was now undecided about just where his future lay. He had time though to think about it, as his results were good – in fact, very good – so knew he could excel in the course he was doing. However, he had the whole summer to confirm what direction he wanted to go in.

Melissa! She was the problem. After what he'd learnt from his parents and his own experiences, he knew he probably hadn't heard the last from her. Melissa had now become his enemy, and she'd probably be unforgiving and vicious – of that he was sure!

Chapter Fifty-One

The journey back to Uni was going well until James found himself stuck at some traffic lights that appeared to be taking an age to change. He looked idly around him when his eyes caught sight of a newsagent billboard stating that a top barrister – a Mr Sebastian John Trelawney – had been seriously hurt in a car crash. He quickly indicated left once the lights had changed and parked along the road. He went back to the newsagents and bought a newspaper. On his return to the car, he settled back into the driving seat and read the article. Apparently, the barrister had suffered a heart attack whilst driving; however, it was reported that he was now in a stable condition and there was optimism for him to make a full recovery.

James was astonished; he'd met this man at the University last year when he was giving a lecture, and James had found him to be a very clever and pleasant man who appeared to know his subject well and was good at lecturing on the topic. The article in the paper gave a résumé of his career, and an idea began forming in James's mind. He would explore the feasibility of it when he got back to Uni.

*

On getting back to his student accommodation, after he'd put everything away then suddenly realised that he was feeling rather hungry after his long drive. *Thank goodness for Mum sending me back with a box of essential supplies,* he thought, then set about making himself an omelette. Afterwards, he sat down with his coffee and decided that, tomorrow, he would go to the Uni library to investigate the firm at which Sebastian Trelawney was a senior partner.

There was a knock on his door, which took him by surprise as he wasn't expecting anyone. James jumped up to answer the door. Finding Melissa standing there, who immediately asked if she could come in. James nodded, she came in and sat down, looking a little uneasy. He had no idea why she was there, so waited for her to start the conversation. He remained standing, leaning against his desk.

"I've come to apologise to you. I think I may have had too much to drink and I'd like to make reparation for my behaviour. Could we meet up somewhere for a drink?" She stopped speaking.

James thought quickly before replying. "I could meet you at The Bistro in Grays Court tomorrow afternoon after 2pm; would that be OK? I have to be at a lecture at 4pm."

Melissa looked startled, but she changed her expression to a smile and agreed to meet then.

James moved towards the door, opened it and said, "See you tomorrow, then," as she went out. He dismissed her from his mind as he had more important things to do, but he did wonder what it was she wanted to say.

*

James spent the next morning in the library, reading all about Sebastian Trelawney's law firm and finally managed to get an appointment with one of the partners, a Mr Ackroyd. He'd created a scenario he wished to discuss with him relating to a project that was part of his third year course. Mr Ackroyd had responded that was happy to meet with James as he was impressed the young man's diligence.

James had just enough time to freshen up before walking to The Bistro to meet Melissa. Once there, he bought a pint of lager and sat down at a table by the window to wait for her.

It was nearing 3pm when she arrived (she'd never been punctual). James stood up as she joined him and asked what she would like to drink.

"Dry white wine," she replied, "Large, please."

James's eyebrows rose; judging by the pink spots on her cheeks and her slightly unsteady gait, he felt she'd already been drinking! Having bought the drinks he brought them back to the table. He waited for her to speak sipping his beer slowly, whilst Melissa chatted about this and that, just making small talk.

Finally, he said, "Would you like another drink?"

She nodded.

James made another trip to the bar, and when he returned, she took a large mouthful of wine saying, "I understand that your mother used to live in London."

James simply replied, "Yes, she did."

"Did she ever meet my mother? After all, your mum was married to Gordon James."

James was puzzled; what was it she was trying to find out? "Yes, my mother had been married to him before she moved to Cornwall, but I have no idea if she ever met or came across your mother though."

Melissa took another large sip of wine and then said in a rush, "I have a claim lodged against the Will of Geoffrey James; he was my father, and part of Simon's Fel belongs to me!" Her expression was one of triumph and bravado as she took another sip of wine and watched as James stood up.

He looked straight at her and, in a steady voice, said plainly and clearly, "You haven't got a hope in hell of getting anything from Simon's Fel." With that, he walked out, his head held high, closing the door quietly behind him.

Melissa's expression turned to fury. She downed the rest of her drink in one go; threw the glass to the floor, smashing it; stood up, knocking the chair over viciously in the process, causing it to break; and then stormed out of The Bistro, slamming the door and using foul language at anyone who got in her way. Once in her car, she raced it out of the car park, its wheels screeching.

The manager rushed after her, noted the registration plate and went straight back in to call the Police. She'd caused him trouble before. His barman took photos on his mobile phone of the damage she'd caused in the bar, which was all reported to the Police when they arrived an hour later, plus there had been plenty of witnesses!

*

Melissa screeched into the car park at the flats, absolutely seething. She'd convinced herself that she was totally in the right and she should be the one who owned Simon's Fel. She threw her coat, bag and shoes across the room, fetched the half empty bottle of wine from the fridge, and drank from that too. Still angry, she opened another one and took it into her bedroom, drinking the entire contents then falling into a druken stupor

*

Two things happened the following morning. Firstly, at 8am, James was called to the Vice Chancellor's office, where a Police Sergeant and a Constable were waiting to see him. All they wanted was confirmation of the previous afternoon's fracas in The Bistro. Having got that, they left politely, with the Vice Chancellor saying nothing other than to assure James that he'd handled the matter really well and there would be no further enquiries.

The second thing that happened that day was to Melissa who woke, turned over and groaned as she noted the time of 9am. Then she remembered how her meeting with James had gone. The feeling of anger rose in her again with the strong urge to put him in his place over what she perceived as her rightful claim. With that, she got out of bed quickly, but as she was feeling a bit hungover, she decided that a quick shower before getting herself dressed would help to clear her head before going out to find James and to confront him with a few home truths as she saw it. So determined was she to find James as soon as possible that she decided she wouldn't bother making herself a coffee, but she'd get one whilst out. As soon as she was showered and dressed, she grabbed her keys, went out the door and headed for her car in the car park.

She was just about to pull away in her car when a police car pulled up in front of her.

A police sergeant got out, approached her and tapped on the car window, indicating that he wished to speak to her. "Are you Melissa Cartwright and the owner of this car?"

"I am, but what's the problem?" replied Melissa.

"The owner of The Bistro you attended last evening has reported you to us and has requested charges of criminal damage be brought against you," he informed her.

"You have to be kidding," retorted Melissa. "What damage?"

"Could you turn off your engine and get out of the car, please," he replied, but then he noticed that there was something off with her demeanour and speech, so he indicated to his colleague to bring him a breathalyser kit. "I have reason to believe, miss, that you may be over the legal limit to drive this car, and I therefore require you to take a breath test." And with that, he handed her the breathalyser unit to blow into.

Melissa was taken aback and was beginning to get irritated. "For goodness' sake, how on earth can I be over the limit at this time of the morning? I haven't had a drink since yesterday!"

"In that case, there shouldn't be a problem, then, so if you wouldn't mind," holding out the unit in front of himself for her to take.

With a huff, Melissa duly submitted to doing the test and was completely aghast when the breathalyser indicated that she was over the drink drive limit. She was promptly arrested and taken to the police station.

She soon realised she was in trouble, but her mind was racing and already working out how she could avoid the charges of drink-driving and criminal damage; after all, she knew enough clever lawyers who could find a loophole in the law. She smiled to herself and waited to hear the worst.

Two hours later, she was back at her flat, grumpy at the scene that met her: empty bottles and clothes strewn around the lounge and her bedroom. *I must have had more to drink than I thought last night,* she thought to herself. She tidied up sulkily, but then started to smile again as she thought about what she'd been charged with, including being over the limit – she was sure she could get away with it! She suddenly felt hungry, then realised that she couldn't remember when she last ate. It was now nearly lunchtime, so she decided she would have some pasta and a nice glass of chardonnay to celebrate.

Chapter Fifty-Two

James decided not to tell his parents about his meeting with Melissa –that could wait for another time! He concentrated on the "project" he was undertaking, trying hard to make it a feasible task for someone studying law. It took him a long time to make his flowchart look professional and informative and to ensure all the necessary information was included. He made notes of possible problems and scenarios that could arise. When he'd finished and put it all together, it looked and read like a proper legal test case. James was pleased all his efforts had come together and hoped his meeting with Mr Ackroyd would be as successful. He then turned to his studies and made sure his last few days at Uni would be very productive.

He arrived at the offices that housed Mr Trelawney and Mr Ackroyd's law firm a little early for his appointment, but it allowed him to watch the comings and goings of the staff. Some were obviously barristers who were either on their way to or from Court. He found it fascinating to see the way these people worked; there seemed to be a real purpose to what they did. His attention was then taken when he heard his name being called out by a middle aged woman, who motioned him to follow her. She led him into a large office, which was comfortable and warm, not only in temperature but also in spirit. She then invited him to make himself comfy in one of the chairs.

Prior to sitting down, he introduced himself and extended his hand to shake that of Mr Ackroyd, at the same time enquiring as to how Mr Trelawney was. Mr Ackroyd acknowledged his greeting and was pleased to say that Mr Trelawney was greatly improved.

"Tell me the general background of your case study," Mr Ackroyd suggested, "then we can work through the various scenarios and possible outcomes."

James gave a background to the case and then explained all his supporting facts; he was really enjoying stating his case and proving his facts. He was gaining confidence the more he spoke and answered Mr Ackroyd's questions as they were put to him. He answered honestly when he didn't know the answer or whenever he wasn't sure of the question. He made notes where needed to ensure those queries could be researched and resolved.

The time went by quickly, and they overran the two hours that had been allotted for the appointment.

Mr Ackroyd took off his glasses and sat back. "I regret to say that we've exceeded our time, Mr Grantley, but it has been very well spent. You have presented your case expertly, and all your facts and arguments have been presented with great knowledge and truth. If I'd been hearing this as an actual case in Court I would have found in favour of the defendant; the claimant, in this instance, has no case in law."

James wanted to cry; he was so relieved for his parents and thrilled that his work had been so well received. He stood up to take his leave of Mr Ackroyd and asked how he should pay for his appointment.

"Don't worry about it Mr Grantley we have great interest in helping students from the University that show enormous aptitude and promise with respect to the legal profession. However, as the firm supports various charities – including bursaries for law students – I can give you a list, and if you wish to make a donation, please do."

Mr Ackroyd accompanied James to the door, and as they reached it, he stopped James. "Just one more thing:may I ask you how many years you've been studying?"

James felt that he must be honest with this man. "Two years, sir."

"Do you have a few minutes to spare?" he asked James, who confirmed that he did.

They both retraced their steps and sat down again. Mr Ackroyd buzzed through to his secretary and requested tea and biscuits. While they were waiting, James answered the questions Mr Ackroyd put to him regarding his background, education and interests. The tea arrived, and it became apparent to James that he had made a very good impression on Mr Ackroyd.

"From having listened to your presentation, I can sense you're dedicated and have pride in all you do, and the way you've worked to achieve what you have in two years at University is highly commendable," Mr Ackroyd declared.

James was stunned; where was this all leading?

"I have a proposition for you. As you know, Mr Trelawney has suffered a heart attack and will have to drastically cut down on his workload in future. I'm now the senior partner following Mr Trelawney's absence and, as such, can make any decisions that can further the integrity of the firm. From what I've observed today, I would like to offer you a trainee position in this firm on completion of your degree. In the meantime, I'd also like to offer you paid work experience; you will be paid a small retainer salary, and all holidays that you currently have from University will be upheld. However, we would expect you to spend at least four days a month in the office during this period, but if you find that you're able to give us more of your time, then obviously, you'll be recompensed accordingly."

James was overwhelmed and speechless. He didn't know how to answer or what to feel. "Thank you so much, Mr Ackroyd; I'm a little in shock! I'll need to talk to my parents, if you don't mind? How soon do I have to let you know my decision?"

"I can give you until the end of July; my secretary will give you all the necessary details on your way out." He stood up again and shook James by the hand, also patting him on the back. "It has been a real pleasure meeting you. I have great hopes for your future at Trelawney's, if you should decide to join us."

James left the office having picked up the information from Mr Ackroyd's secretary, who had it ready to pass to him (*How did she know?* he thought), leaving his own details with her. He was too keyed up and excited to go straight back to his Uni digs, so he returned to his car, put more money on the parking ticket, then went and found a coffee shop to sit down in to sort out his thoughts and the enormous opportunities that had been put his way.

Chapter Fifty-Three

James called his parents and had a long conversation with them. They were thrilled to hear the news about Simon's Fel, and then astounded at how impressive James had been and what it had led to.

"I have until the end of July to decide and to give Mr Ackroyd my decision, so I'll put it all on hold until I come home. I miss you all, and I'm looking forward to seeing you." James then ended the call home, as he needed to get some sleep because he was exhausted. He would be glad to get home, but he still had work to do – even more so now.

Abe and his team were working flat out to try to get Pops' Place ready before Justin and Carla's wedding. All the men worked long hours, leaving their wives to deal with the wedding preparations.

Janine was getting more and more excited as the

days went by, and in the end, Jeannie sent her off to make herself useful by helping Lucy to get the bedrooms ready for Gino and Marie (Carla's parents), plus for Seb and Bryan (his flatmate) who would arrive two weeks later. Janine was happy with this, feeling particularly thrilled at the idea that she was cleaning and tidying what would be Bryan's room. At least, with Lucy, she was happy to do anything that was asked of her, as being like most youngsters of today, she found herself always arguing with her mother.

Everyone was making an effort to have most things ready so they could all go shopping and enjoy the day. The men had already decided to wear their existing best suits for the wedding, so it was only the women who had lots to buy, and they were all looking forward to it.

$$*$$

James arrived home and went straight into working at The Tavern; he soon got back into the swing of it. He knew he needed to speak to his parents about his future and had decided that this weekend would be the right time. As he came home from The Tavern, the light was still on in the cottage, so he called in to confirm that his parents would have time on Saturday morning to have a chat.

"That's fine, Son; we'll ask Jeannie and Janine to have the children so we won't be disturbed," his dad offered.

James declined a hot drink and went straight to bed; he was feeling very tired as so much had happened. He just needed to finalise things.

---
*

The next morning, Janine came to collect the children; she was going to take them to see Pops' Place and then for an ice cream. James watched them go and went straight over to the cottage. His mind was now settled – he knew what he wanted to do.

"Mum, Dad, before you ask any questions, I just want you to know I've decided to accept Mr Ackroyd's offer," he explained. "I'm also going to start my new venture of writing children's storybooks and getting them published, or at least have a go at it. Wish me luck on both!"

Simon and Felicity looked at each other, then they both hugged him.

"We're so pleased for you, James, and wish you all the best. Now sit down so we can ask you some questions,"

A few hours later, James was on duty at The Tavern when Melissa walked in. James was shocked, for she'd lost weight, her hair was unkempt and she hadn't made any attempt with her appearance. "Hello, Melissa, what would you like to drink?"

"I'll have a wine. White wine."

"Large?" James replied, and then, as he turned to get a glass of wine for her, he thought to himself, *Your manners certainly haven't improved.*

"I expect you heard about my suspended sentence and driving ban, of course. Also, they've asked me to leave the University, citing that I was a bad influence and my behaviour was disruptive."

James didn't reply as a customer came in, so he went over to serve that person first. When he got back, her glass was empty. "Another?" he asked.

She nodded.

He poured one, handed it to her and took her money. "How did you get here if you've been disqualified?"

"I drove myself here," she snapped. "I bought a new car and registered it in your name!"

"You did what?" he said as he felt the anger rising in him. He turned away from her and went straight to the phone to ring home. "Dad, I need help; Melissa's here and she's driven herself in a new car that she's registered in my name, but she's banned from driving!" As he put the phone down, he noticed that she'd gone from the bar, so there was nothing he could do.

Michael was on his way to Heathrow, so James couldn't leave Lucy on her own to cope as she was covering for Michael in the kitchen.

A few minutes later, Simon rushed through the door. "Where is she?" Simon enquired as he looked around the bar.

"She's gone, Dad; what do I do now?"

Without saying anything Simon rushed past James and was soon talking urgently and firmly on the phone. A few minutes later, he was back in the bar. He'd phoned the Police and had given them all the information; hopefully, they would soon pick her up.

"Thanks, Dad, I was at a loss to know what to do. Can I get the car de-registered at the DVLA?" James questioned.

"The Police are going to get back to me when they've managed to stop Melissa; we'll ask them then what we need to do. See you later, James." With that, Simon headed back home.

A few moments later, the inn's phone rang; it was Justin on his mobile.

James answered it. "It's James, Justin; where are you all?"

"Hi James, we're coming through Exeter at the moment, so we should be with you in about two hours. I'm looking forward to seeing you all!"

James popped his head around the kitchen door and gave the news to Lucy; he was needed in the bar so couldn't stay to chat.

The time flew by with a late flurry of customers, and the next thing James knew, the car was pulling up outside, and its weary passengers getting out, stretching their limbs as they came into The Tavern. Lucy rushed out from the kitchen, so happy to see them all. They were all travel weary but so happy to have arrived at last. Michael sorted out the luggage and took Gino's and Maria's up to their room, while Carla's and Justin's would go on to Abe and Jeannie's after they'd had a welcoming drink – they were all thirsty. Fortunately, it was quiet in the bar so James had the chance to greet them all. He was also looking forward to when Seb and Bryan would arrive.

*

Half an hour later, Michael took Carla and Justin to Abe and Jeannie's house, where Janine was jumping up and down with excitement. Jeannie gave them supper immediately, and shortly afterwards, she showed them to their room for some well earned rest.

*

Later still, Michael shut the doors of The Tavern as soon as the last customer had left. James explained briefly about Melissa and informed him that Simon had dealt with it, but he hoped all would be OK. James then left and went home to his cabin. He was settled with his life, his hopes for his career appeared to be working well, and with luck, Melissa should soon be totally out of the picture .

From tomorrow, the wedding plans would start in earnest; it was going to be a great summer!

Chapter Fifty-Four

Melissa had gone back to the University to clear out the remainder of her belongings. So, as it was now the summer break, she had plenty of time to sort things out with no one about, giving her time to decide what she would now do with her life.

She had conveniently forgotten all about the criminal charges she was facing and the fact that she'd been expelled from the University. Somehow, her expectations were that she would be judged not guilty and be exonerated from any wrong doing!

She was still angry with James. Nothing had worked in her favour, and she'd convinced herself that it was all his fault. She stomped about in her uni room, her anger building as she packed her boxes. Suddenly, she stopped, an idea forming in her mind. The more she thought about it, the more she realised it could work! Hastily, she finished her packing, left the University and headed home.

Once back at her flat she made plans, this time she

would make sure they wouldn't be thwarted. It took her well into the night to formulate them. There was much to arrange, including a visit to Simon's Fel, as she knew she could gain access to James's cabin when they were all at the wedding, having recalled what the day's arrangements would be from the conversations she'd overheard on her previous visits. It would be easy, so easy, for her to get the information she needed. She even knew where they kept the spare key for James's cabin. She was feeling very pleased with herself and had even decided to dye her hair and get it cut into a short style, that way, she felt no one would recognise her. She even bought a second-hand car for cash from a backstreet dealer who was quite happy with the name and address she gave him, which, of course, was false. She drove away quietly, mentally hugging herself; this time she was sure she would succeed!

*

The time was fast approaching for Justin and Carla's wedding. Everything had been arranged, so Michael and Lucy had invited everyone from the village to The Tavern for drinks the evening before the wedding. Justin was staying at Simon's Fel that night, and they would then all go together to the wedding venue the next day. Justin had held a small stag do in Middle Trenchard, and Carla had arranged a small hen party at The Hobby Loft.

Seb and Bryan had arrived a few days before and had been really excited to see everyone. They had even joined the gang trying hard to complete Pops' Place, which they managed to do with one day to spare! That event was very special and prompted yet another impromptu party. It was turning out to be a very special time for everyone.

*

The wedding day dawned. The weather was lovely, and as they all walked through the village to the church, no one noticed the small, scruffy car being driven along the road by a young woman with short, blonde hair.

Chapter Fifty-Five

The wedding party was a great success and went on well into the evening. Justin and Carla left for a mini honeymoon in Cornwall without telling anyone where they were going! The rest of the guests carried on partying, until they finally left at midnight.

James stayed behind to help Lucy and Michael to clear up, and then he joined Seb and Bryan in their room for a good chat to catch up. It was really late, or rather the early hours of the morning, when James got back to his cabin, he was surprised to find the door unlocked, but he assumed he may have forgotten to lock it due to so much happening that day and everyone being busy. He had a quick look around and all appeared to be OK, so he went off to bed, completely exhausted from the effort of the day but happy that all had gone so well.

It wasn't until he got up late the next morning that he noticed some of the papers on his desk appeared to have been re-arranged. He was puzzled over it, but he couldn't work out why he had such an uneasy feeling from looking at how things were lying on his desk. Maybe he'd just forgotten how things had been left? It was the work he'd done prior to the meeting with Mr Ackroyd. He sighed, shrugged his shoulders and set about tidying up the papers; he concluded that he must still be tired from yesterday. He was due at The Tavern at noon, so now wasn't the time to worry over something that seemed so incidental.

"James? James? Are you still at home?" He heard his mother calling to him a short while later, so he quickly left the cabin, locked his door and went across to the cottage.

She had just wanted to check if he was going to be in for dinner later; however, he told her that he would be meeting up with Seb, Bryan, Dave and Stan for a boys' night out, so not to worry, plus, it was likely he'd be home late. He went off to The Tavern, looking forward to the evening ahead, forgetting completely about his earlier concerns.

*

Seb and Bryan were staying in Little Trenchard for another two weeks, then they would be going back to New Zealand. Carla's parents were going back with Justin and Carla at the end of the week. Everyone else were busy making plans to visit New Zealand the following year, hoping that they could go for a month!

Things had been so busy that James hadn't had the time to spend sorting out the things he would be needing for his coming year at University. He'd kept in touch with Mr Ackroyd to confirm his trainee position and the time he needed to fulfil his contract. He didn't think about Melissa and just assumed that she'd disappeared from his life. At last, after the New Zealand residents had left to go back, he had time to spare to prepare for his return to University.

James sat at his desk to sort out all his papers, including the test case he'd spent so much time preparing for his interview with Mr Ackroyd. How fortunate that had proved to be! He frowned as he went through the papers again, some were in the wrong order and a couple of the pages were missing. He frowned again and then decided to ring Mr Ackroyd. He soon got through and explained what he needed help with. Within an hour, Mr Ackroyd had sent him an email. Thank goodness James had possessed the foresight to record the test case on a memory stick!

James finished his packing in readiness for his return to University, including putting together the test case papers in their entirety, containing all the information needed to answer the queries that arose from Mr Ackroyd. He was still puzzled as to why some pages had gone missing, but he couldn't think of any plausible reason.

*

That evening, James was having supper with his parents because he was planning to leave for Bristol in the morning.

As he went into the cottage, Simon handed over an envelope which had arrived earlier that day. "It's postmarked Bristol and came this morning; it could be important, Son."

James took the envelope, opened it and took out the letter inside. On reading it, his face drained of colour, and he sat down abruptly. He passed the letter to his father.

"Read it, Dad," he said, "Melissa has accused me of plagiarism."

Chapter Fifty-Six

Simon and James left for Bristol the next morning. The evening before, they'd sat down together and thoroughly discussed the accusation Melissa had made. It appeared that she'd stated she had written a paper on Inheritance Law and was accusing James of stealing her ideas and thoughts, and then using them to gain employment with the well known firm of Trelawney's, using *her* work as his test case.

Simon had been so angry, with all his dislike of lawyers coming to the fore again. Felicity calmed him down and persuaded him to accompany James to the University, as he'd been "invited" to attend a meeting with the Dean and Vice Chancellor.

Prior to them leaving, James called Mr Ackroyd to inform him of the letter and the accusations. He had the full backing he needed, plus a promise that Trelawney's would give any help or assistance required to enable him to refute the allegations. James also realised that the memory stick could prove his innocence; the files on it were dated, and all the pages, graphs and diagrams were numbered.

James and Simon set off in good spirits, sure that they could show James had not committed plagiarism. They were due to meet the Dean and Vice Chancellor at 2pm, however, as they had made such good time getting to Bristol, it allowed them enough time for lunch.

At precisely 2pm, the Dean's secretary ushered them into his office. Once the pleasantries were over, the Dean invited James to state his position regarding the charges made against him by Melissa. James responded clearly and concisely about what had occurred, what he had prepared for his test case, and whom he'd been to see for the assessment of the case. The Dean's eyebrows rose when the name of Trelawney's was mentioned, particularly that it was Mr Ackroyd who had listened to the case.

Simon had kept quiet throughout the interview, feeling surprised, proud and impressed at the way his son presented himself with such confidence.

The Dean stayed silent for a while, but he then rang through to his secretary with the request that she ask the Vice Chancellor to join them. When he arrived, the Dean took him into a side office so they could speak privately, leaving Simon and James alone with their thoughts.

As they returned from the side office, the Dean introduced the Vice Chancellor. "This matter needs further investigation following on from what you've stated. Also, the Vice Chancellor has received an email from Mr Ackroyd which confirms the details of your test case. He's coming to the University to present the evidence, and following that, our decision will be made. However, in the meantime, you may remain in the halls of residence at the University to continue your studies."

"Thank you very much, sir; I'm fully prepared for the next part of my course." James stood up, shook hands with both men and went out, smiling and motioning to his father to follow him.

Somewhat bewildered, Simon followed James, and as they left the building, he said, "What did that all mean, James?"

Smiling again, James replied, "All's well, Dad; they're letting me stay. Melissa has lost her case against me."

Chapter Fifty-Seven

Simon settled into his seat in the train carriage as he travelled home alone, mulling over all that had happened at the University. He realised there was nothing further they could do except wait for the decision from the Dean. He turned his thoughts back to the family at home; Simon's Fel was secure, he was contented and happy with Felicity, and he had a lovely family waiting for him back home, so life was good.

When he arrived at Exeter Station, Abe was waiting for him and had several bits of news to impart as he drove them home. Bella had gone into premature labour, but had been safely delivered of a daughter. Jeannie had immediately taken charge of Matthew, so Stan was able to be with Bella until the baby was out of danger. They'd been assured all was well at the moment, and the doctors were optimistic that she could go home soon. Dave and Vanessa had confirmed that they were expecting a second baby too. As it turned out they were having twins! Lucy and Michael had decided they would retire in five years' time and wanted Stan and Dave to build them a bungalow for their retirement. So much had happened in such a short space of time.

When they arrived back in Little Trenchard, Abe stopped at Simon's Fel, as Felicity had invited him, Jeannie, Janine and little Matthew for dinner. Simon was so pleased to see his family, safe, sound and secure. Felicity wanted to be reassured that all was well with James, so Simon briefly told her that James was fine and he'd explain everything later.

It was a lively evening between the two families, their long friendship having been cemented over time.

Bella was OK and staying at the hospital until their daughter was able to be brought home. Stan was back at work, but he managed to spend some time with Matthew every evening before he went to see Bella and their baby. Janine took to bathing Matthew in the evenings, happy to be part of the proceedings.

Dave approached Abe to ask if there was any way they could extend their part of the house, as their family was growing and they would eventually need the space. Abe was immediately thrilled to be asked to help and happy to have yet another project to manage. He would talk to Jeannie; maybe they could sell that part of the house to Dave and Vanessa, and then make it into a pair of semi-detached houses. Dave was happy to see what Abe could plan, knowing whatever he thought of would be appropriate. Their future looked good, work was plentiful and contentment was bountiful.

---
*

Life was busy over the next few months with the plans and paperwork to facilitate Dave and Vanessa's new extension and the splitting of one house into two. Further plans were started for a retirement bungalow for Lucy and Michael. Also, a coming-home party was being organised for Bella and Stan's baby daughter, who was now doing well and thriving. They named her Rebecca Jane, though she was known to Matthew as "BB" (short for "baby Becca"), which was all he could say.

Lucy and Michael had news of their own: Justin and Carla were expecting their first baby. The proud grandparents-to-be were thrilled and excited at the prospect, and they hoped that they could time their next trip to New Zealand to coincide with the baby's arrival. It seemed that everything was going so well for them all.

However, at the back of his mind, Simon was still worried about James and the spectre of Melissa. He kept his thoughts to himself, Felicity was busy with the children and The Hobby Loft, so he didn't want to upset her with his concerns. James rang regularly; his studies and work experience were going extremely well, and he came home as often as he could. Neither Felicity nor Simon ever asked if he had a girlfriend, his experience with Melissa was still too raw.

The following evening, James rang and was pleased it was his father who answered the phone. "Dad, I have some news that I need to tell you straight away: Melissa has gone missing. The police came to see me this afternoon and wanted to know if I knew where she was; obviously, I don't, and I told them so. Briefly, in her absence, she was fined and banned from driving for two years; on top of that, she was also convicted of criminal damage; and following the accusations she made against me, she was also found guilty of theft and fraud." James stopped to gather his thoughts, then went on, "The Court also took into account her purchase of the car that she bought in my name, which she drove without insurance. There's more to explain, but I'll tell you that when I see you next, which by the way, will be Friday for the weekend. Oh, and will you tell Mum that I'll be there for dinner. Love to you all! I have to go." With that, the phone went dead.

Simon stared at the receiver as though he was expecting it to speak.

"Was that James?" Felicity asked as she came into the sitting room.

"Yes, it was," Simon confirmed, somewhat bemused. He then explained to Felicity everything James had said ending with, "He'll be home on Friday, and he hopes to arrive in time for dinner."

Chapter Fifty-Eight

James arrived late on the Friday afternoon. The children were highly delighted and clambered all over him, being so pleased to see their big brother, plus they all wanted to know what he'd brought home for them. They went away happy with the sketch pads and crayons that he pulled out of his backpack for them, with an admonishment to them to only use the pads for drawing on! He greeted his parents warmly and said he would talk to them later when the children were in bed; in the meantime, he would settle into his cabin, he had a lot to do.

His studies were going really well and his work experience with Trelawney's was even better than he'd expected. Mr Ackroyd had personally chosen to take him under his wing. James was learning so much from him. They had a good working relationship, and James's confidence was growing under the excellent guidance of Mr Ackroyd. He loved the work and was intrigued with all the intricacies of law and its ultimate consequences. He was contented, happy, sure in his choice of career and lucky to have a good family life too.

James read bedtime stories to his siblings to settle them down for the night before having a chat with his parents.

He joined them in the living room and began: "Melissa has just gone missing. The police are trying to trace her as there are legal matters that need to be settled, which she must face. I don't know exactly what they are, as just when the police visited me to ask if I knew of her whereabouts, they didn't say. Mind you, I don't care to know, as I'm just glad she's out of my life now." James stopped for a moment.

Felicity and Simon waited for him to continue, sure there was more to come.

"The strange thing is," he continued, "that a couple of days before she went missing, I received a large package in the post; it was full of papers relating to the block of flats that Melissa's mother had left her. It was delivered by hand, so it had no sender address on it – just a label with my initials on it. I handed it over to the police for them to deal with. They thought it was probably information about the rentals of the block of flats that Melissa now owns. I took a copy of the papers, just in case this information is useful to us at all in the future."

James sat back in the armchair, smiling at his parents. "Hopefully, nothing will come of it, but it does seem strange. I'll leave the papers with you for safekeeping, but maybe, when you have time, you could take a look at them and see what you make of it? In the meantime, Dad, how do you feel about going for a pint?"

Simon was all too ready to agree, so the two of them set off for The Tavern.

Felicity watched them go, pleased that they were happy to be out together. She was intrigued about the papers James had received. What could they show? She went up to her sitting room, smiling as she looked at the painting of Simon she'd done so many years ago. It still thrilled her to look upon the image she'd painted; she'd really caught the silvery glints in his eyes! With a start, as she looked more closely at the painting, she was seeing, as if for the first time, how much James looked like his father. With the same tilt to his head, his stance, his hair and those glints to his eyes, he was so very much like his father, and had his nature too. She was very proud of her son.

After settling down with the folder, Felicity read through the papers, but she couldn't understand a lot of the legal phraseology in them and was puzzled as to why they had been sent to James. She sighed heavily and put them aside; she would speak to Simon later, and they could then decide if it was worth trying to find out if they were important. Meanwhile, there were more important things to deal with: the party to welcome Bella and Rebecca home, the new bungalow for Lucy and Michael, and Dave and Vanessa's extension. Over the other side of the world, there was the happy news of another new life to look forward to in the shape of Justin and Carla's baby!

Chapter Fifty-Nine

It was a very busy summer in the village that year. Michael had managed to secure a plot of land for their retirement bungalow, which was on the outskirts of the village and within walking distance of their friends. The plans for dividing Abe and Jeannie's house had been granted, as had the planning permission to extend the property. Dave and Vanessa had decided to name their new home The Other Half, much to the amusement of Abe and Jeannie, who had always referred to that part of the property as that anyway when Bella and Seb had lived there! Abe took on the task of overseeing the project with great delight as he was enjoying working closely again with Dave and Stan.

Everyone in the village had been invited to Bella and Rebecca's homecoming; it would be a great celebration. Greetings had been received from New Zealand, and Seb was especially disappointed that he was unable to be there in person. However, a promise was made that he would be back in Cornwall following the family visit later that year.In the meantime, he and Bryan had been planning their future.

So much was happening that it was hard to keep track of it all! The extension of The Other Half was well underway, the initial plans had been submitted for Lucy and Michael's bungalow, and they were now putting ideas together to plan for the future of The Tavern.

James was excelling at Uni and had managed to pass all his exams earlier than expected with a distinction, plus his work experience with Trelawney's had secured him the offer of a trainee solicitor placement at the firm, which he was delighted to accept. He was going to spend the summer running The Tavern for Lucy and Michael, along with the ever faithful Sandra in the bar. Mr Ackroyd had agreed he could commence his employment and traineeship at the beginning of October, but James would need to undertake University studies for the additional course he wanted to do on a part-time basis until he'd completed it. James knew it would be hard work, but it was what he wanted. It meant he would also have to find time to pursue his other love, as he still had plans to publish his photos and sketches in books for children.

Foremost in the minds of Lucy and Michael was the forthcoming visit to New Zealand and the birth of their first grandchild. Their plans were underway. Janine was going with them, and they would spend the whole summer holiday with Justin and Carla, although her parents had insisted that they stay with them as they had more space at their home. The surprising thing was that Seb and Bryan proposed to come back to England with them afterwards! Emails and phone calls were flying back and forth until all plans were in place. It took a while, but at last, everything was organised.

*

Bella and Stan had settled well with Rebecca, and young Matthew loved having a little sister around. He was fascinated by her and couldn't wait until she was old enough to run around with him.

It had been a few weeks before Bella found she had the time to spare to finish sorting through all the old papers they'd found in the loft when it was being cleared before they started the rebuild of Pops' Place. As Matthew was to spend the day with her parents, it left her with Rebecca, who was sound asleep. Taking the baby monitor with her, Bella went into the small box room, which was going to be turned into a bolt hole for her. She sat down and started to work her way through the boxes of papers. Having gone through through several of them, which were mostly old receipts, bills and guarantees from long gone items, she stood up and stretched, then realised she'd lost track of time and as she was now feeling hungry. She decided to take a break and get some lunch, plus she needed to check on Rebecca.

Once she'd fed Rebecca and had some lunch herself, she went back to the box room to continue her task, taking the baby with her. After settling Rebecca into her rocker, Bella went back to the next box of papers to sort through.

Within this next box, she came across an envelope stuffed with old photos. As she went through them, she became really excited to find pictures of people who must have been part of Ray's family. Shuffling through them, she came across one photo of someone who looked as though it could be Ray when he was a small boy. Eagerly, she turned it over to see if there was any information written on the back, but unfortunately, Rebecca was starting to get unsettled, so Bella packed up the pile of photos to give her daughter the attention she was needing.

Later on, she took Rebecca to her parents' home and spent time with them before going back home to bathe and feed the children. Once they were in bed, she had dinner with Stan.

It was a little later in the evening before she had time to return to the photographs she'd found. Meanwhile, Stan had gone out to see Dave and Abe for a progress report on The Other Half, which had left her to have the evening to herself and the chance to peruse the pictures. Sometime later, doing just that, Bella picked up the phone, dialled the number she wanted and waited for an answer.

"Hello, Felicity here."

"I'm glad you answered; are you able to come over to Pops' Place straightaway? Stan's out, so I can't leave the children. Is Simon at home?" Bella's tone sounded urgent.

"Yes, of course," Felicity answered, "so I can be with you shortly. Are you OK, Bella?"

"I'm fine, thanks, Felicity, but there's something here I've found that I think you should see."

Chapter Sixty

Felicity arrived at Pops' Place within a few minutes of Bella's phone call. She was worried about the urgent tone in Bella's voice, but when she arrived, she was taken by surprise at how warmly and calmly Bella greeted her, invited her into the living room, and offered coffee and biscuits which Felicity accepted. While she relaxed sipping her coffee, Bella then went to get what she wanted to show her.

As it appeared there was nothing to worry about, Felicity took the opportunity to look around the room. *How lovely it is*, she thought, *and what a beautifully comfortable home Bella and Stan have created.*

Bella came back into the room and handed Felicity some photos and old papers, saying, "Look at these; I was astonished when I found them and thought you should see them straightaway. They could be important; I just hope they won't come as too much of a shock!"

Felicity took the package that was handed to her and started leafing through the stack of papers and photos, looking startled and then tearful, even occasionally exclaiming out loud. After she had gone through them twice, she turned to Bella. "Thank you for finding these and letting me see them; I can't quite understand it all!" She stopped and took a deep breath. "I think the gist of it all was that the woman who was a servant in Geoffrey James's house, having been raped by him, found herself pregnant and cast out as a result, was Melissa's mother and Ray's sister."

Bella nodded. "That's what I understood too; it seems that Ray was unaware of his sister's existence until he found out not long before he died. She had obviously been trying to trace him and did find him eventually, but as far as I could make out, she never met him."

Neither Bella nor Felicity spoke for a while as the startling information was hard to take in and to understand.

Finally, Felicity declared, "We need to find out exactly what all of this means and how it might affect us, as the implications could be manifold!"

Bella got up and went to make more coffee. On her return, they both settled down to think through the next steps they needed to take in the quest to find out the full story of this extraordinary information Bella had unearthed.

After a lot of thought and searching through all the papers and photos again, they devised a plan to search for the necessary information to confirm the identity of Melissa's mother. They agreed to split the research between them, and they decided to involve Jeannie and, particularly, Lucy. They both agreed it could be a great shock to Lucy as she may not be aware that she and Ray had a sister. Felicity made a mental note to have a word with James, as he may have some ideas about the legal implications of it all!

Felicity left Bella just as Stan arrived home. Having had a productive meeting with Abe and Dave, he was in a cheerful mood.

When Felicity got home, Simon was snoozing in her sitting room.

He greeted her happily with a hug and settled her on his lap. "Did you two have a good chat together this afternoon, and was it worthwhile?"

Felicity was very quiet; Simon frowned and started to worry, but then she sighed heavily before relating everything she'd just learnt to Simon.

Bella was also telling Stan about the papers and the information she'd found. Stan was intrigued at first, but then he too was concerned at the possible implications of it all.

Both men, after having been told, had one thought: What will Melissa do if and when she finds out? Or does she already know? And if so, how much? After all, she has put in a claim for Simon's Fel.

Chapter Sixty-One

When James had found out from his mother about Ray's previously unknown sister, his immediate reaction had been to call Mr Ackroyd and ask his advice. It took some time to collate all the information. Felicity, Bella and Jeannie had contacted the General Register Office to submit an application for information on births, marriages and death records appertaining to the family. They also put in a search on a couple of the ancestry search sites, which they hoped would assist them to find the appropriate Parish, Church or census records to indicate which district or area to look in to trace Ray's family background. That would at least point them in the direction of where archived records of old workhouses and orphanages were now stored (if that was to be relevant in their search). In fact, they were trying anything they could think of. Even Janine got involved, having come up with the idea of checking old school records!

*

All this was happening while the normal life of the village carried on. The building projects were progressing well: Dave and Abe had almost finished work on The Other Half, and Stan had moved on to preparing the ground for Lucy and Michael's bungalow. Dave and Vanessa were expecting their twins to arrive soon, and James had finished at Uni. He was back home now and preparing to take over as landlord of The Tavern while Michael and Lucy were away in New Zealand.

At the beginning of August, Abe, Jeannie and Janine, accompanied by Lucy and Michael, were all leaving for New Zealand; they would all be away for a month. Justin and Carla had moved into a new apartment, which was much bigger and better, and also nearer to Justin's office in the middle of Auckland. Everyone was excited to see their respective relatives, especially for a whole month. Lucy and Michael were particularly looking forward to the birth of their first grandchild.

Justin was astonished to hear of the turn of events about Ray and his other sister; he hadn't known anything about it and was concerned that his mother hadn't known anything either. He resolved to investigate and search any websites that may furnish them with any information; he had a great deal of IT knowledge, which may throw up some leads. Meanwhile, their baby was due soon, the family were arriving, and it was going to be a good summer. He and Carla were going to surprise everyone with the news that they were planning a trip to Little Trenchard for Christmas, bringing Gino and Marie with them too, as they'd enjoyed themselves so much last time that they wanted to visit again.

Simon and Felicity had promised to keep them all updated on the progress of their research into the saga of Ray's sister, whenever they had new information to report.

Seb and Bryan had finished their University courses, having both gained their qualifications as accountants. They had plans to start a business together to audit accounts for small businesses, but it was still in the initial planning stage. However, they were determined to follow it through as they'd identified a need in the market for it.

*

The family arrived in New Zealand to great excitement. Justin and Gino were going to pick them all up at the airport, but at the last minute, Carla had gone into labour, so Gino got Marie to take Justin's place to help with picking everyone up.

By the time they arrived at Marie and Gino's house, the baby had arrived. There was a message on the phone, so Gino and Marie went straight to the hospital, with Seb having been despatched to greet the family. Abe, Jeannie and Janine were delighted to see him; he looked so well and was equally thrilled to see them all. Lucy and Michael decided immediately that they should raise a glass to the baby, so they opened the bottle of champagne that Seb had thoughtfully brought along. Justin had been so excited when he had left the phone message that he'd forgotten to say if it was a boy or girl! They raised a glass to the baby anyway, so it was a very happy crowd that greeted Marie and Gino a couple of hours later. Justin was staying at the hospital for the evening with his wife and new baby daughter.

At dinner time, another bottle of champagne was opened, Marie produced a huge pan of spaghetti bolognese to feed everyone, and they all partied well into the night.

Seb had to leave to assist Bryan at the bar where they worked, but he did so with a promise that they would both be back to spend the weekend with the whole family. As he was about to leave, he cornered his dad and said, "We have something to discuss with you, Mum, Lucy and Michael. It's important, Dad, and we would appreciate your thoughts." He went out without waiting for an answer.

Puzzled, Abe decided to wait until he and Jeannie were on their own before mentioning it, Seb had been smiling when he spoke to me, so it could only be something good, he thought.

Chapter Sixty-Two

They all got up late the next morning as it had been so exhausting and exciting the previous day. Justin arrived at Gino and Marie's just after lunch, much to the delight of everyone, bringing photos of his daughter. Lucy and Michael were thrilled, and Janine decided she would title herself an honorary aunt!

Justin stayed for the afternoon, then went home to prepare for Carla and the baby's homecoming the following day. They hadn't yet decided on a name for the baby; they were just so pleased all had gone well with the birth and that both were doing great. Lucy and Marie were going off to do some baby shopping, and Janine asked eagerly if she could go too. They agreed, and she happily jumped into the car with them, thrilled to be able to accompany them. The rest of the family spent a happy afternoon lazing in the warm sunshine and recovering from jet lag. Both Abe and Jeannie speculated about what Seb and Bryan wanted to discuss.

Halfway through the afternoon, the phone rang.

Gino answered it and then turned to Jeannie. "It's Felicity for you."

Jeannie jumped up at once, took the phone from Gino, and listened intently occasionally saying,"Yes," or,"No," until, finally, she finished by saying, "Justin and Carla have a daughter; they'll be coming home tomorrow. We're all fine. Speak to you soon; give our love to everyone."

She put the phone down and turned to face the others. "The latest news is that there was indeed a third child, Ray and Lucy's sister." Jeannie stopped to gather her thoughts.

Gino stood up and suggested, "I think I should leave you alone to discuss this because it feels as if it's obviously private information about your family in Cornwall."

Abe and Jeannie said immediately that he should remain, after all, he was now part of the family. He sat down again.

Jeannie continued, "It appears that a couple of years before Ray was born, his father had a child with another woman, but he hadn't known she was pregnant when the relationship ended. Ray and Lucy's father then went on to marry their mother. The other woman gave birth to a daughter, but the mother had died in childbirth. The baby was raised in an orphanage, and she then later went into domestic service."

Jeannie stopped briefly to have a drink. "This has all been found out from the research they have conducted. Felicity said there's a lot more to it, but she's only given me a shortened version! However, they did find out that this woman had been employed by Geoffrey James, and he had raped her. She had then been cast out and gave birth to a daughter, who turned out to be Melissa's mother!"

No one spoke for a while.

Then Gino got up. "I'll go make some coffee for us all. Thank you for letting me join in with you. If there's anything we can do to help, please let us know." He went off to the kitchen.

As he did so, the door opened, and Janine burst in carrying several shopping bags. "We've bought some lovely things for the baby, and I even bought something for Matthew and Rebecca, and for Grace too!" She was so excited and pleased, everyone smiled at her enthusiasm.

Time was then spent examining the baby clothes and toys.

Marie managed to say, "Justin rang a bit earlier to say that they want us to bring Lucy and Michael to the hospital, so you can visit Carla and the baby this evening. We'll go at about 5pm, and then Justin will join us later for dinner." She smiled happily at everyone.

Lucy and Michael were thrilled. Janine offered to help with preparing the dinner that her mother was going to get ready for everyone later.

Lucy went upstairs, and Jeannie followed her to let her know about Felicity's phone call, telling her that Abe was downstairs filling Michael in too.

Lucy sat down abruptly and went very pale at the news. She looked at Jeannie. "This is a real shock.

I had absolutely no idea; none at all. I do know that Ray had become interested in our family history, so that must have been the papers that Bella found. We'll put this aside for the moment, Jeannie; we're here to celebrate." She then hugged Jeannie and shed a few tears, commenting, "I'm so glad you're here!"

Jeannie left to go and start the preparations for dinner. Lucy, meanwhile, shed a few more tears when Michael came to join her. He hugged her tightly, not saying anything, just giving her the comfort she needed. There was a lot to talk about, but that could wait as they were shortly going off to see their granddaughter.

Chapter Sixty-Three

Back in Little Trenchard, there was a great deal of discussion taking place about the discovery of Ray's family history, which Felicity and Simon had spent a considerable amount of time compiling, followed by putting together a family tree to try and make sense of it all. Felicity let Jeannie know what they'd been doing, and Lucy confirmed that they would wait until they returned before they got too involved, as after all, they did want to enjoy their time with the family in New Zealand.

James hadn't heard anything more from the police about Melissa's disappearance; it seemed as though she'd just vanished! He did have some concerns about her possible reaction to the information being uncovered about her heritage. Mr Ackroyd was still exploring the possible implications that could affect them all.

Felicity took some time away from all the research to take the children down to The Hobby Loft for the day, where she sat them all down with pencils, crayons, paper and sketch books to have fun being creative. While the children were occupied, she took the opportunity to do a stock check on the equipment and materials they would need prior to her opening the premises again in the September.

When it got to lunchtime, she'd prepared a special treat for them all of a "floor picnic" at The Hobby Loft. To make it fun, she laid out a picnic blanket on the floor for them, then set out little coloured plates for them to eat their sandwiches and biscuits off, completing the special treat with a beaker of fizzy lemonade each.

The ringing of the phone startled her, and she immediately jumped up to answer it, albeit a little worried as to who it could be!

"Help me, please, Felicity; I can't get hold of anyone else. Grace is crying, and I don't know what to do! I started bleeding. It's stopped now, but I'm scared!" It was Vanessa, and Felicity could hear the panic in her voice.

"Ring for an ambulance, and then unlock the door so I can get in. I'll be there in about five minutes." She put the phone down, and then told the children to leave everything where it was and to come with her straight away. She ushered them out of the door locking it behind her, before hurrying off to help Vanessa.

True to her word, she was with Vanessa within five minutes. But by the time she got there, she found Vanessa was distraught as she was two months away from her due date; on top of that, Grace was fretting because her mummy was crying. Picking up Grace to settle her, Felicity then checked that Vanessa had called for an ambulance, and then she rang Ruth (who attended her classes) and asked her if she could come and help her with the children.

The paramedics arrived shortly, with lights flashing, and they took charge of the situation immediately. Felicity found milk and biscuits to keep the children quiet, as they hadn't had time to finish their picnic lunch, and at that point, Ruth arrived. As the children knew her as because she was one of their neighbours in the village, they were quite happy to go with her. She took custody of them straight away and took them all off to Simon's Fel. On her way out the door with the children, Ruth assured Felicity that she would stay with them for as long as it took until she returned.

Having arranged all that she could, Felicity then went to see how Vanessa was doing and found that she appeared to be more settled now, having been given a sedative to calm her down.

"We have to take Vanessa to the hospital urgently, as it would appear she may need to have an emergency Caesarean section, one of the paramedics explained. "We've alerted the hospital and shall be taking her there now. May we please ask you to contact her husband? She's fretting that she can't get hold of him. Also, would you let us have your name and telephone number as a means of contact for us for the moment?"

Felicity gave them her details and told them that she would get to the hospital as soon as she could. The paramedics advised her that they would be taking her to the Royal Devon and Exeter Hospital , and within two minutes, they were on their way with Vanessa, their ambulance's lights flashing and siren wailing.

Felicity sat down to gather herself and her thoughts, then she got up quickly, locked up Vanessa's home behind her and rushed off to Simon's Fel.

*

The children were all pleased to see her, they'd been wondering what was happening. Ruth had them all settled down and was prepared to stay as long as needed, which Felicity was grateful for as it meant she could get together a bag of necessities to take to Vanessa. She phoned James quickly to let him know what was happening and requested he call his Dad to let him know, but the first thing she told him he should do was to get in touch with Dave as soon as possible. As soon as she finished speaking to James, she gathered up the bag of items she'd put together for Vanessa and left to go to the hospital in Exeter, hoping that James was able to get hold of Dave and his father to inform them of the situation without delay.

En route to the hospital, Felicity's mobile rang, which she quickly answered hands-free in her car. Dave was stunned, having just got James's message. She told him to get to the hospital in Exeter immediately, as it was likely that Vanessa had been taken straight to a theatre on arrival there.

"I'm on my way there now," he told her before he rang off, sounding very worried and concerned for his wife.

Ten minutes later, Felicity arrived at the hospital and went straight to the neonatal department of the maternity wing, where she was advised at the enquiry desk that Vanessa wasn't back from the theatre yet; however, they could tell her that she'd been delivered of two live babies. Both were very small but able to breathe on their own OK. With that, she sat down in the waiting area and burst into tears of overwhelming relief. She had received several phone calls, as Simon, Bella and Stan had all called her.

Dave rushed in through the doors, and she gave him a quick hug before he was taken immediately in to see Vanessa and the babies.

Somewhat at a loss, Felicity wondered whether she should stay or go home, so she decided to hand over the bag of necessities she had brought along for Vanessa and then go home as she felt there was nothing further she could do. She was just making her way out of the unit when she heard her name being called. Turning, she saw Dave rushing up to her.

He hugged her with tears in his eyes. "Thank you so much; you saved the day. Vanessa is OK, and we have twin boys, both of whom seem to be well, but they have to stay in incubators for a while. Thank you so much! I'll come and collect Grace later if that's OK? But I'd be grateful if you could keep her with you for a bit longer?"

"Oh, Dave, of course. Take your time; she'll be fine with us. Give our love to Vanessa, and congratulations on your boys. Take all the time you need, and if there's any further help you need, please just let me know."

Exhausted, Felicity left the hospital and drove home, thankful that all had turned out OK. As she drove into the drive at Simon's Fel, she suddenly remembered the mess she'd left behind at The Hobby Loft! *No worries. That can all wait until tomorrow to be sorted!* she thought.

Chapter Sixty-Four

As soon as he heard their car pull into the driveway, Simon went to the door to greet Felicity as she got home. He hugged her, and then sat her down and brought her a large glass of wine.

She was still tearful; *It's probably delayed shock* she thought as she had a sip of wine.

"We've sorted everything out. Ruth has now gone home; she was brilliant with the children, and they loved being with her. Bella came over to say that she and Stan had cleaned up the lounge after Vanessa went to the hospital, so everything has been tidied up over there. Ruth even took charge of Matthew and Rebecca! Bella also packed a bag for Vanessa with everything she'll need, as its likely she'll be in hospital for a while. I called Dave a short while ago and told him we'd have Grace stay with us for as long as needed, to help them out. I hope that's OK with you?"

Felicity burst into tears again, so thankful that her worry had been lessened so much. "Thanks so much.

You have been busy! That's such a weight off my mind, plus it'll give huge relief and peace of mind to Vanessa and Dave that Grace will be taken care of. I'm so glad their boys are doing OK, and thank goodness The Other Half was finished before Abe and Jeannie went to New Zealand. Oh! It's just dawned on me that we must get in touch to let them know what's happened."

"It's OK, darling; I've sent an email as the time difference wouldn't be conducive to us phoning them in what would be the early hours of the morning." He smiled at her again.

Just then, the children erupted into the kitchen. "Mummy," they all called out and went to hug her.

"Has Nessy had her babies? And when is she bringing them home?" asked Cassie.

They were all clambering over Felicity asking her so many questions all at once; the most important one being when they were going to be fed.

Simon fetched Grace as she had just woken up, and not knowing where she was, she'd started to cry. He handed Grace to Felicity, so she could comfort the little one, then turned immediately to the others. "Who wants beans and fishfingers?"

They all crowded around him, but he shooed them off to go and wash their hands before sitting down while he prepared their tea. Meanwhile, Felicity was putting together a feed for Grace.

A short time later, while the youngsters were all eating, Simon took the opportunity to fetch the old cot from the loft, give it a good clean and retrieve the bedding for it from the top of the airing cupboard. He was making it as comfortable as he could for Grace, although he was sure Felicity would give everything the once over before putting her to sleep in it.

By the time Felicity got all the children ready for bed, settled and asleep, it was getting quite late; however, by the time she got back downstairs she found that Simon had rustled up a pasta dish for their evening meal.

Felicity sighed heavily as she thought of the mess that was left at The Hobby Loft, plus the checklist she was preparing, and she wondered aloud how she'd fit in dealing with everything along with looking after the children, including Grace.

Simon, as if reading her thoughts, looked at her and said, "I'll sort all that; you just concentrate on seeing to the children tomorrow, and consider The Hobby Loft done. I'll bring back all your lists, and you can finish them at home."

They were both starting to relax when there was a knock at the door; it was James. He walked in carrying a box of papers, which he handed to his father. "I won't stop long, Dad, I just wanted to hand you these. Mr Ackroyd sent them, and they could be useful. The gist of his investigations are that he doesn't think there's any way that a claim could be made against Ray's estate. I have the evening off tomorrow, so I'll come over then; dinner would be good too!" Looking at his mother, he smiled and winked on his way out the door to make his way to the cabin, tired but content.

Felicity and Simon looked at each other; there were no words that could explain how proud they were of James.

Chapter Sixty-Five

The events of the last week had taken its toll on everyone; however, they'd all managed to settle into a routine. Vanessa was recovering well, and the twins had been moved to a premature baby unit; whilst they were thriving, they weren't as yet ready to be discharged for home.

The news of their birth had been relayed to New Zealand, and everyone would all be home at the end of next week. As yet, Dave and Vanessa hadn't chosen any names for their twins, but Justin and Carla had eventually decided to call their daughter Rosemary Anne, and they were hoping to have her christened in Little Trenchard when they came over at Christmas time.

Seb and Bryan had invited Lucy, Michael, Abe and Jeannie to join them for a "consultation" to discuss an idea they had which was currently in its infancy. However they needed to put their idea to all four of them to know if they thought it would be feasible. Once everyone was together, Seb nervously cleared his throat before starting to speak. "Dad, Mum, Lucy and Michael. Bryan and I have been discussing our future, and we've thought long and hard about this. We both have our accountancy qualifications and would like to open our own business dealing with the accounts and auditing for small businesses. We could run this from a small office, and it would involve the two of us doing everything ourselves, so we wouldn't need to employ any staff. But to go alongside this, we'd like to have our own bar or small pub as well." As he said this, he looked at Lucy and Michael to see if he could gauge their reaction.

Bryan carried on from Seb: "Seb and I have gained experience of running a bar since being here, so we feel we're fully qualified and knowledgeable in that area. To that end, our idea is that we purchase The Tavern from you and run it as a bar and restaurant, having our own apartments in the accommodation above, which would, of course mean ending the B&B part of the business." He stopped speaking and looked at the astonished faces staring at him.

"Are you really serious about this, Son?" asked Abe.

"Yes, Dad, we are; we think it's feasible as there's plenty of room to convert the living accommodation into two apartments plus an office. We just need your thoughts and permission to do it." He looked at Lucy and Michael, who were still sitting there silently, as he was waiting for their reaction.

"It isn't anything we had thought about," Michael said, looking from Seb and Bryan to Lucy, as if to get confirmation from her of what he was about to say, "As we're only currently in the first stages of having our retirement bungalow built, we had considered selling the pub and using the proceeds to be our retirement fund." He looked at Bryan and Seb. "My immediate thought was of Justin, but that really is of no matter, as he'll inherit the bungalow, so who buys the pub is immaterial. But the idea of someone we know buying it is somehow appealing." He turned to Lucy. "What do you think, darling?"

Lucy looked back at them all. "I'm astounded; it wouldn't have occurred to me, but I think it's a great idea!"

All eyes then turned to Jeannie, as she hadn't yet said a word. So many thoughts had been going through her head, but the main one was that her son would be coming home! Tears glistened in her eyes. "I think it's a great idea!"

Everyone then started to talk at once, but Abe declared finally, "We must all approach this properly and with professional help. It will be a big project and require a lot of planning in the first instance. If you lads are serious about this, we can make a start when we get home from New Zealand and set the project in motion."

Chapter Sixty-Six

Lucy and Michael talked long into the night; both were excited and enthusiastic about Seb and Bryan's proposal. They also had a long conversation with Justin; he too was enthusiastic with the idea and assured his parents that, as his future life was now set in New Zealand, he was happy to accept whatever they decided.

Abe and Jeannie were thrilled at the thought that Seb would be coming home and entering into a great business partnership opportunity with Bryan. Bryan himself hadn't had a happy childhood, having been orphaned in his early teens, and he'd needed to work hard to make his own way in life. For him, meeting Seb had been a turning point in his life as it had given him a firm friendship and confidence in himself that had enabled him to make a success of his life. The camaraderie of Seb's family had been a new concept to him at first, but they'd been so warm and friendly in welcoming him into their midst that it didn't take too long for him to feel part of the family, which was such a good feeling.

They were all looking forward to going back to Little Trenchard, with so much about to happen, there would be a lot to do and to plan. There was a great deal to look forward to once they got home, what with new babies to meet and now new projects to look forward to.

Janine was secretly pleased; in fact, she was highly delighted that Bryan was coming to live in Little Trenchard. She still liked him a lot and hoped that he'd begin to notice her when they moved from New Zealand.

James was thrilled his friend was coming back home; he too was looking forward to the future. He had secured his position with Trelawney's, plus he'd collated the photos and sketches for his first children's book on wildlife, in readiness for publication. He hadn't as yet thought of a title, but he knew something appropriate would come to him in time.

The only thing that still concerned him was Melissa's disappearance. Nothing more had been heard of her – or from her. However, by making some discreet enquiries to one of the leaseholders at the block of flats Melissa owned, he'd found out the name and address of the agents who were dealing with the management of the property. But when James contacted the agents to request the landlord's contact details, he was advised by them that all their instructions came via a company registered in the Cayman Islands, and so they had no direct contact with the landlord at all, nor did they know of any way to contact her.

Where had she gone and why? He was fairly sure that they hadn't seen the last of her.

*

Meanwhile, on her balcony overlooking the sparkling waters in the bay, past the little whitewashed village below, with a cup of coffee in hand and taking in the scene in front of her, Melissa was mentally finalising her plans.

"Ray may have influenced my mother in some way when she was alive, but he's no longer around to stop me…!"

This book is printed on paper from sustainable sources managed under the Forest Stewardship Council (FSC) scheme.

It has been printed in the UK to reduce transportation miles and their impact upon the environment.

For every new title that Troubador publishes, we plant a tree to offset CO_2, partnering with the More Trees scheme.

For more about how Troubador offsets its environmental impact, see www.troubador.co.uk/sustainability-and-community